She was like ... kissed.

She was sodden ... trace of make-u ... every which way. There were trickles of rainwater running down her nose, merging with the rain on his face where their lips met. She looked about as far from his ideal woman as he could possibly imagine any woman being.

So how could she be meeting this need—this desperate desire that until now he'd never known he had?

Marion Lennox was born on an Australian dairy farm. She moved on—mostly because the cows weren't interested in her stories! Marion writes Medical Romance™ as well as Tender Romance™. Initially she used a different name for each category, so if you're looking for past books, search also for author Trisha David.

In her non-writing life Marion cares (haphazardly) for her husband, teenagers, dogs, cats, chickens and anyone else who lines up at her dinner table. She fights her rampant garden (she's losing) and her house dust (she's lost). She also travels, which she finds seriously addictive.

As a teenager Marion was told she'd never get anywhere reading romance. Now romance is the basis of her stories; her stories allow her to travel, and if ever there was an advertisement for following your dream, she'd be it! You can contact Marion at www.marionlennox.com.

Recent titles by the same author:

TO THE DOCTOR: A DAUGHTER (Medical Romance™)
A MILLIONAIRE FOR MOLLY (Tender Romance™)
DR BLAKE'S ANGEL (Medical Romance™)
A ROYAL PROPOSITION (Tender Romance™)

STORMBOUND SURGEON

BY
MARION LENNOX

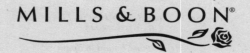

This book is dedicated to Chloe,
my writing companion for the last twelve years.

Every author needs one totally dedicated fan, and without
her big heart and wet nose my books would be the poorer.

*MILLS & BOON and MILLS & BOON with the Rose Device
are registered trademarks of the publisher.*

*First published in Great Britain 2003
Harlequin Mills & Boon Limited,
Eton House, 18-24 Paradise Road, Richmond, Surrey TW9 1SR*

© Marion Lennox 2003

ISBN 0 263 83454 9

*Set in Times Roman 10¼ on 11¼ pt.
03-0703-48945*

*Printed and bound in Spain
by Litografia Rosés, S.A., Barcelona*

PROLOGUE

THE lawyer cleared his throat and looked miserable. This was nothing short of blackmail, and the girl before him deserved so much better.

But the old man finally had her where he wanted her. Robert Fleming had manipulated people all his life. The only person who'd broken free had been his stepdaughter, and now he was controlling her from the grave.

The will was watertight. Fleming would succeed and there wasn't a thing the lawyer could do about it.

'Just read it,' Amy said, stony-faced. The lawyer collected himself. And read.

'To my stepdaughter, Amy Freye, I leave my home, White-Breakers. I also leave her the land on Shipwreck Bluff and sufficient funds to build a forty-bed nursing home. The home is to be built in the style of a resort, to ensure resale is possible, and I set aside the following to be invested for maintenance...

The above bequest is conditional on Amy living permanently in Iluka for at least ten years from the time of my death. If she doesn't fulfill this condition, White-Breakers and the nursing home are to be sold and my entire estate is to be divided evenly between my nephews. The nursing home is to be sold as a resort for holiday-makers who'll appreciate Iluka. As Amy never has.'

CHAPTER ONE

'IF IT doesn't stop raining soon I'll brain someone.' Amy put her nose against the window and groaned. Outside it was raining so hard she could barely see waves breaking on the shoreline fifty yards away.

'Great idea. Brain Mrs Craddock first.' Kitty, Amy's receptionist, was entirely sympathetic. 'If I hear "Silver Threads" one more time I'll do the deed myself.'

It was too late. From the sitting room came the sound of the piano, badly played, and Mrs Craddock's warbling old voice drowned out the television.

'Darling, we are getting old,
Silver threads among the gold...'

Murder was looking distinctly appealing, Amy decided. 'Can you taste arsenic in cocoa?' she muttered. 'And just what are the grounds for justifiable homicide?'

'Whatever they are, it can't be more justifiable than this. A week of rain and this lot...'

It was the limit. Nothing ever happened in Iluka, and this week even less than nothing was happening. The locals jokingly called Iluka God's Waiting Room and at times like this Amy could only agree.

It did have some things going for it. Iluka was a beautiful seaside promontory with a climate that was second to none—apart from this week, of course, when the heavens were threatening another Great Flood. It had two golf courses, three bowling greens, magnificent beaches and wonderful walking trails.

6

On the cliff out of town was Millionaire's Row—a strip of outlandishly expensive real estate. At the height of summer the town buzzed with ostentatious wealth.

But the rest of the time it didn't buzz at all. Iluka was a retiree's dream. The average age of Iluka's residents seemed about ninety, and when the rain set in there was nothing to do at all.

Nothing, nothing and nothing.

Card games. Scrabble. Hobbies.

Lionel Waveny had made five kites this month and he hadn't flown any of them. The sitting room was crowded at the best of times, and if he made one more kite they'd have to sit on them.

From the sitting room came excited twittering. 'Amy... Bert's won.'

Great. Excitement plus! Summoning a smile Amy headed into the sitting room to congratulate Bert on his latest triumph in mah-jong. She stepped over Lionel's kites and sighed. She really should stop him making them but she didn't have the heart. They were making him happy. *Someone* should be happy. So...

'Great kite,' she told Lionel, and added, 'Hooray,' to the mah-jong winner. 'Bert, if you win any more matchsticks you can start a bushfire.'

Despite her smile, her bleak mood stayed.

Oh, for heaven's sake, what was wrong with her? she wondered. What was a little rain? This was a decent sort of life— wasn't it? The nursing home she'd set up was second to none. Her geriatric residents were more than content with the care she provided. She could start a cottage industry in knitwear and kites, she had a fantastic home—and she had Malcolm.

What more could a girl want?

Shops, she thought suddenly, and a decent salary so she could enjoy them. She stared down in distaste at the dress she'd had for years. What else? Restaurants. A cinema or two, and maybe a florist where she could buy herself a huge bunch of flowers to cheer herself up.

Yeah, right. As if she'd ever have any money to buy such things.

She looked out the window at the driving rain and thought...

What?

Anything. Please...

Amy wasn't the only one to be criticizing Iluka. Five miles out of town Joss Braden was headed for the highway and he couldn't escape the town fast enough.

'It's the most fantastic place,' his father had told him over the phone. 'There's three separate bowling greens. Can you believe that?'

'Yes, but—'

'Now, I know bowling doesn't interest you, boy, but the beaches are wonderful. You'll be able to swim, catch lobster right off the beach and sail that new windsurfer of yours. Go on, Joss—give us a few days. Get to know your new step-mother and have a break from your damned high-powered medicine into the bargain.'

He'd needed a break, Joss thought, but five days of rain had been enough to drive him back to Sydney so fast you couldn't see him for mud. For the whole week his windsurfer had stayed roped to the car roof. The seas had been huge—it would have been suicidal to try windsurfing. His father and Daisy had wanted him to spend every waking minute with them; they'd been blissfully and nauseatingly in love, and medicine was starting to look very, very good in comparison.

So this morning, when the newsreaders were warning of floods and road blockage, his decision to leave had bordered on panic. Now he steered his little sports car carefully through the rain and crossed his fingers that the flooding wasn't as severe as predicted.

'Ten minutes and we're on the highway and out of here,'

he told his dog. His ancient red setter, Bertram the Magnificent, was belted into the passenger seat beside him, staring through the windscreen with an expression that was almost as worried as his master's. If they were stuck here...

'We'll be right.'

They weren't.

'Amy, love, we need a fourth at bridge.'

'I'm sorry, Mrs Cooper, but I'm busy.'

'Nonsense, child. We know you always go for a walk on the beach mid-morning. You can't walk anywhere now, so come and join us.'

'But I can't play.'

'We'll give you hints as we go along. You'll be an expert in no time.'

Aargh...

Once they reached the highway it'd be easier.

The road into Iluka from the highway twisted around cliffs along the river. It was a breathtakingly scenic route but it was dangerous at the best of times, and now was the worst possible time to be driving.

Joss's hands gripped white on the steering-wheel. He leaned forward, trying to see through the driving rain, and his dog leaned forward with him. Bertram's breath fogged the windscreen and Joss hauled him back.

'There's no need for both of us to see.'

It'd be better once they were on the highway, he told himself. Just around this bend and across the bridge and...

His foot slammed hard on the brake.

Luckily he was travelling at a snail's pace and the car's brakes responded magnificently. He came to a halt with inches to spare. But inches to what? Joss stared ahead in disbelief. He had to be seeing things.

He wasn't. Ahead lay the bridge. The water was up over

the timbers in a foaming, litter-filled torrent, and the middle pylon was swaying as if it had no base.

And as Joss stared, there was a screech of tortured metal, a splintering of timber and the entire bridge crumbled and buckled into the torrent beneath.

'I can't play bridge. I've promised to help Cook make scones.'

'Oh, Amy...'

Beam me up, someone. Please beam me up...

Joss opened the car door with caution. He was safe enough where he was but seeing a bridge disappear like that made a man unsure of his own footing. Thankfully the ground underneath felt good and solid, even if a relentless stream of water began to pour down his neck the minute he opened the door.

Before him was a mess. The entire bridge was gone. In the passenger seat Bertram whimpered the unease of a dog in unfamiliar territory, and Joss leaned in to click the seat belt free.

They weren't going anywhere fast, Joss thought grimly. Bertram was a water dog at heart, and if Joss was going to drown out here at least he'd have happy company.

'Stupid dog. You can't possibly like weather like this.'

He was wrong. Joss even managed a grin as Bertram put his nose skywards, opened his mouth and drank.

But his humour was short-lived. How was he to get back to Sydney now?

First things first, he told himself. Before he started to panic about escape routes, he needed to do something about oncoming traffic. He didn't want anyone plunging unaware into that torrent.

He bent into the car again and flicked his lights to high beam. The river wasn't so wide that oncoming cars wouldn't see his warning. Then he flicked on his hazard lights.

But his warning was too late. A truck came hurtling around the bend behind him and it was travelling far too fast. Above the roar of the river Joss hardly heard it coming, and when he did he barely had time to jump clear.

The smash of tearing metal sounded above the roar of the water. There was a crashing of broken glass, a ripping, tearing metallic hell, and then the sounds of hissing steam.

Joss backed away fast and Bertram came with him.

What the...?

His car had been totalled. Just like that.

He swallowed a few times and laid a hand on his dog's shaggy head, saying a swift thank you to the powers who looked after stupid doctors who ventured out in sports cars that were far too small. In a world where there were trucks that were far too big. In weather that was far too bad.

Then he took in the damage.

The other vehicle looked like an ancient farm truck—a dilapidated one-tonner. If Joss's sports car had been bigger it would have fared better, but now... His rear wheels were almost underneath his steering-wheel. The passenger compartment where Joss and his dog had sat not a minute before was a mangled mess.

Hell!

'Stay,' he told Bertram, and thanked the heavens that his dog was well trained. He didn't want him any closer to the wreck than he already was. The smell of petrol was starting to be overpowering...

He had to reach the driver.

Damage aside, it was just as well his car had been where it was, Joss thought grimly. Coming with the speed it had, if Joss's car hadn't been blocking the way the truck would now be at the bottom of the river.

If anyone else came...

There was another car now on the other side of the river, and it also had its lights on high beam. Joss's lights were still working—somehow. The lights merged eerily through the rain and there was someone on the opposite bank, waving wildly.

They'd all been lucky, Joss thought grimly. Except—maybe the driver of the truck.

The smell of petrol was building by the minute and the driver of the truck wasn't moving. Hell, the truck's engine was still turning over. It only needed a spark...

The truck door wouldn't budge.

He hesitated for only a second, then lifted a rock and smashed it down on the driver's window. Reaching in, he switched off the ignition. The engine died. That'd fix the sparks, he thought. It should prevent a fire. Please...

Were there injuries to cope with? The driver was absolutely still. Joss grabbed the handle of the crumpled door from the inside and tried to wrench it open. As he worked, he lifted his phone and hit the code for emergency.

'The Iluka bridge is down,' he said curtly as someone answered, still hauling at the door as he spoke. 'There's been a crash on the Iluka side. I need help—warning signs and flashing lights, powerful ones. We need police, tow trucks and an ambulance. I'm trying to get to the driver now. Stand by.'

'If you won't play bridge how about carpet bowls?'

'That's a good idea.' At least it was active. Amy was climbing walls. 'Let's set it up.'

'But you'll play bridge with us tomorrow, won't you, dear? If it doesn't stop raining...'

Please, let it stop raining.

'You're wanted on the phone, Amy.' It was Kitty calling from the office. 'It's Chris and she says it's urgent.'

Hooray! Anything to get away from the carpet bowls—but the local telephonist was waiting and at the sound of her voice, Amy's relief disappeared in an instant. 'What's wrong?'

'I don't know.' Chris was breathless with worry. 'All I got

was that the bridge is down. There's been a crash and they want an ambulance. But, Amy, the ambulance has to come from Bowra on the other side of the river. If the bridge is down... If there's a medical emergency here...'

Amy's heart sank. Oh, no...

Iluka wasn't equipped for acute medical needs. The nearest acute-care hospital was at Bowra. The nearest doctor was at Bowra! Bowra was only twenty miles down the road but if the bridge was down it might just as well be twenty thousand.

'I don't know any more,' Chris told her. 'There was just the one brief message and the caller disconnected. I've alerted Sergeant Packer but I thought...well, there's nowhere else to take casualties. You might want to stand by.'

It was a woman and she was in trouble.

Joss managed to wrench the door open to find the driver slumped forward on the steering-wheel. Her hair was a mass of tangled curls, completely blocking his view. She was youngish, he thought, but he couldn't see more, and when he placed a hand on her shoulder there was no response.

'Can you hear me?'

Nothing. She seemed deeply unconscious.

Why?

He needed to check breathing—to establish she had an airway. He stooped, wanting to see but afraid to pull her head back. He needed a neck brace. If there was a fracture with compression and he moved her...

He didn't have a neck brace and he had no choice. Carefully he lifted the curls away and placed his hands on the sides of her head. Then, with painstaking care, he lifted her face an inch from the wheel.

With one hand holding her head, cupping her chin with his splayed fingers, he used the other to brush away the hair from her mouth. Apart from a ragged slash above her ear he could feel no bleeding. Swiftly his fingers checked nose and throat. There was no blood at all, and he could feel her breath on his hand.

What was wrong?

The door must have caught her as it crumpled, he thought as he checked the cut above her ear. Maybe that had been enough to knock her out.

Had it been enough to kill her? Who knew? If there was internal bleeding from a skull compression then maybe...

She was twisted away from him in the truck, so all he could see was her back. He was examining blind. His hands travelled further, examining gently, feeling for trauma. Her neck seemed OK—her pulse was rapid but strong. Her hands were intact. Her body...

His hands moved to her abdomen—and stiffened in shock. He paused in disbelief but he hadn't been mistaken. The woman's body was vast, swollen to full-term pregnancy, and what he'd felt was unmistakable.

A contraction was running right through her, and her body was rigid in spasm.

The woman was in labour. She was having a baby!

'Amy?'

'Jeff.' Jeff Packer was the town's police sergeant—the town's only policeman, if it came to that. He was solid and dependable but he was well into his sixties. In any other town he'd have been pensioned off but in Iluka he seemed almost young.

'There's a casualty.' He said the word 'casualty' like he might have said 'disaster' and Jeff didn't shake easily. Unconsciously Amy braced herself for the worst.

'Yes?'

'It's a young woman. We're bringing her in to you now.'

'You're bringing her here?'

'There's nowhere else to take her, Amy. The bridge is down. We'd never get a helicopter landed in these conditions and Doc here says her need is urgent.'

'Doc?'

'The bloke she ran into says he's a doctor.'

A doctor... Well, thank heaven for small mercies. Amy let her breath out in something close to a sob of relief.

'How badly is she hurt?'

'Dunno. She's unconscious and her head's bleeding. We're putting her into the back of my van now.'

'Should you move her?'

'Doc says we don't have a choice. There's a baby on the way.'

A baby.

Amy replaced the receiver and stood stunned. This was a nursing home! They didn't have the staff to deliver babies. They didn't have the skills or the facilities or...

She was wasting time. Get a grip, she told herself. An unconscious patient with a baby on the way was arriving any minute. What would she need?

She'd need staff. Skilled staff. And in Iluka.... What was the chance of finding anyone? There were two other trained nurses in town but she knew Mary was out at her mother's and she didn't have the phone on, and Sue-Ellen had been on duty all night. She'd only just be asleep.

She took three deep breaths, forcing herself think as she walked back out to the sitting room.

Thinking, thinking, thinking.

The vast sitting room was built to look out to sea. Mid-morning, with no one able to go outside, it held almost all the home's inhabitants. And they were all looking at her. They'd heard Kitty say the call was urgent and in Iluka urgent meant excitement.

Excitement was something that was sadly lacking in this town. These old people didn't play carpet bowls from choice.

Hmm. As Amy looked at them, her idea solidified. This was the only plan possible.

'I think,' she said slowly, the solution to this mess turning over and over in her mind, 'that I need to interrupt your carpet bowls. I think I need all hands on deck. Now.'

Fifteen minutes later, when the police van turned into the nursing home entrance, they were ready.

Jeff had his hand on his horn. Any of the home's inhabitants who hadn't known this was an emergency would know it now, but they were already well aware of it. They were waiting, so when the back of the van was flung wide, Joss was met by something that approached the reception he might have met at the emergency ward of the hospital he worked in.

There was a stretcher trolley rolled out, waiting, made up with mattress and crisp white linen. There were three men— one at each side of the trolley and one at the end. There was a woman with blankets, and another pushing something that looked blessedly—amazingly—like a crash cart. There was another woman behind…

Each and every one of them wore a crisp white coat and they looked exceedingly professional.

Except they also all looked over eighty.

'What the…?'

He had barely time to register before things were taken out of his hands.

'Charles, slide the trolley off the wheels—that's right, it lifts off. Ian, that's great. Push it right into the van. Push it alongside her so she can be lifted… Ted, hold the wheels steady.…'

Joss glanced up from his patient. The efficient tones he was hearing weren't coming from a geriatric. They came from the only one in the group who didn't qualify.

She was a young woman, nearing thirty, he thought, but compared to her companions she was almost a baby. And she was stunning! She was tall and willow slim. Her finely boned face was tanned, with wide grey eyes that spoke of intelligence, and laughter lines crinkled around the edges that spoke of humour. Her glossy black hair was braided smoothly into a long line down her back. Dressed in a soft print dress with a white coat covering it, she oozed efficiency and starch and competence. And…

Something? It wasn't just beauty, he thought. It was more…

'I'm Amy Freye,' she said briefly. 'I'm in charge here. Can we move her?'

'I… Yes.' Somehow he turned his attention back to his patient. They'd thrown a rug onto the van floor for her to lie on. It wasn't enough but it was the best they could do as there'd been no time to wait for better transport. The thought of delivering a distressed baby in the driving rain was impossible.

'Wait for me.' Amy leaped lightly into the van beside Joss. Her calm grey eyes saw and assessed, and she moved into action. She went to the woman's hips and slid her hands underneath in a gesture that told Joss she'd done this many times before. Then she glanced at Joss, and her glance said she was expecting matching professionalism. 'Lift with me. One, two, three…'

They moved as one and the woman slid limply onto the stretcher.

'OK, fit the wheels to the base,' the girl ordered of the two old men standing at the van door. 'Lock it into place and then slide it forward.'

In one swift movement it was done. The stretcher was on its wheels and the girl was out of the van.

'Take care of the dog, Lionel,' she told an old man standing nearby, and Joss blinked in astonishment. The top triage nurses in city casualty departments couldn't have handled things any better—and to even notice the dog… He opened his mouth to tell Bertram things were OK, but someone was handing towels to the man called Lionel, the old man was clicking his fingers and someone else was bringing a biscuit.

Bertram was in doggy heaven. Joss could concentrate on the woman.

'This way,' Amy was saying, and the stretcher started moving. Doors opened magically before her. The old men beside the stretcher pushed it with a nimbleness which would have been admirable in men half their age, and Joss was left to follow.

Where was he? As soon as the door opened, the impression of a bustling hospital ended. Here was a vast living room, fabulously sited with three-sixty-degree views of the sea. Clusters of leather settees were dotted with squashy cushions, shelves were crammed with books, someone was building a kite that was the size of a small room, there were rich Persian carpets...

There were old people.

'Do we know who she is?' Amy asked, and Joss hauled his attention back where it was needed.

'No. There was nothing on her—or nothing that we could find. Sergeant Packer's called in the plates—he should be able to get identification from the licence plates of the truck she was driving—but he hasn't heard back yet.'

She nodded. She was stopping for nothing, pushing doors wide, ushering the stretcher down a wide corridor to open a final door...

'This is our procedures room,' she told Joss as she stood aside to let them past. 'It's the best we can do.'

Joss stopped in amazement.

When the police sergeant had told him the only place available was the nursing home he'd felt ill. To treat this woman without facilities seemed impossible.

But here... The room was set up as a small theatre. Scrupulously clean, it was gleaming with stainless-steel fittings and overhead lights. It was perfect for minor surgery, he realised, and his breath came out in a rush of relief. What lay before him started looking just faintly possible.

'What—?'

But she was ahead of him. 'Are you really a doctor?' she asked, and he nodded, still stunned.

'Yes. I'm a surgeon at Sydney Central.' But he was focussed solely on the pregnant woman, checking her pupils and frowning. There didn't seem a reason for her to be so deeply unconscious.

He wanted X-rays.

He needed to check the baby first, he thought. He had two patients—not one.

'You can scrub through here.' Amy's face had mirrored his concern and she'd followed his gaze as he'd watched the last contraction ripple though her swollen abdomen. 'Or...do you want an X-ray first?'

'I have to check the baby.' She was right. He needed to scrub before he did an internal examination.

'I'll check the heartbeat. The sink's through here. Marie will help.'

A bright little lady about four feet high and about a hundred years old appeared at his elbow.

'This way, Doctor.'

He was led to the sink by his elderly helper—who wasn't acting elderly at all.

There was no time for questions. Joss was holding his scrubbed hands for Marie to slip on his gloves when Amy called him back.

'We're in trouble,' she said briefly, and her face was puckered in concern. She'd cut away the woman's smock. 'Hold the stethoscope here, Marie.' Then, with Marie holding the stethoscope in position over the swollen belly, she held the earpieces for Joss to listen.

His face set in grim lines as he heard what she'd heard. 'Hell.' The baby's heartbeat was faltering. He did a fast examination. The baby's head was engaged but she'd hardly dilated at all. A forceps delivery was still impossible. Which meant...

A Caesarean.

A Caesarean here?

'We don't have identification,' Amy was saying. 'Will you...?'

That was the least of their worries, he thought. Operating without consent was a legal minefield, but in an emergency like this he had no choice.

'Of course I will. But—'

'We have drugs and equipment for general anaesthetic,' she finished, moving right on, efficient and entirely professional in her apology. 'The Bowra doctor does minor surgery here, but I'm afraid epidural is out of the question. I...I don't have the skills.'

After that one last revealing falter her eyes met his and held firm. They were cool, calm, and once again he thought that she was one in a million in a crisis.

'What's your training?' he started, hesitating at the thought of how impossible it would be to act as anaesthetist and surgeon at the same time—but she was before him there, too.

'Don't get the wrong idea. I'm not a doctor,' she said flatly. 'I'm a nurse. But I'm qualified in intensive care and I spent years as a theatre nurse. With only one doctor in the district, I've performed an emergency general anaesthetic before. That's why we have the drugs. For emergencies. So if you guide me, I'm prepared to try.'

He stared at her, dumbfounded by her acceptance of such a demand. She was a nurse, offering to do what was a specialist job. This was a specialist job for a qualified doctor!

But she'd said that she could do it. Should he trust her? Or not?

He hardly had a choice. He'd done a brief visual examination on the way here. The baby was still some way away—the head wasn't near to crowning—and now the baby's heartbeat was telling its own grim story. If they waited, the baby risked death.

He couldn't do a Caesarean without an anaesthetic. The

woman was unconscious but the shock of an incision would probably wake her.

He needed a doctor to do the anaesthetic, but for him to perform the Caesarean and give the anaesthetic at the same time was impossible.

Amy wasn't a doctor. And she was offering to do what needed years of medical training.

But... 'I can do this,' she said, and her grey eyes were fearless.

He met her gaze and held it.

'You're sure?'

'Yes.'

'You realise insurance...'

'Insurance—or the lack of it—is a nightmare for both of us.' She nodded, a decisive little movement of her head as though she was convincing herself. 'But I don't see that we can let that worry us. If we don't try, the baby dies.'

It went against everything he'd ever been taught. To let a nurse give an anaesthetic...

But she was right. There was no decision to be made.

'OK. Let's move.'

It was the strangest operation he'd ever performed. He had a full theatre staff, but the only two under eighty years old were Amy and himself.

Marie stayed on. The old lady had scrubbed and gowned and was handing him implements as needed. Her background wasn't explained but it was assumed she knew what she was doing, and she handled the surgical tray with the precision of an expert.

And she had back-up. Another woman was sorting implements, moving things in and out of a steriliser. A man stood beside her, ready with a warmed blanket. Every couple of minutes the door opened a fraction and the blanket was replaced with another, so if—when—the baby arrived there'd be warmth. There was a team outside working in tandem, ferrying blankets, hot water, information that there was no chance of helicopter evacuation…

Joss took everything in. He checked the tray of instruments, the steriliser, the anaesthetic. He measured what was needed, then sized Amy up.

'Ready?'

'As ready as I'll ever be.' Still that rigid control.

He looked at her more closely and saw she was holding herself in a grip of iron. There was fear…

It would help nothing to delay or probe more deeply into her fear, he decided. She'd made a decision that she could do it and she had no choice. There was no choice!

'Let's go, then.'

Amy nodded. Silently she held her prepared syringe up so he could check the dose. He nodded in turn and then watched as she inserted it into the IV line.

He watched and waited—saw her eyes move to the monitor, saw her skilfully intubating and inflating the cuff of the endrotracheal tube, saw her eyes lose their fear and become intent on what they were doing.

He felt the patient's muscles relax under his hand.

She was good, he thought exultantly. Nurse or not, she knew what she was doing, which left him to get on with what he had to do.

He prepped the woman's swollen abdomen, lifted the scalpel and proceeded to deliver one baby.

CHAPTER TWO

IT WENT like clockwork.

This team might be unusual but their competence was never in question. As he cut through the abdominal layers the old woman called Marie handed over instruments unasked. When Joss did need to ask, her responses were instantaneous.

And Amy's anaesthetic was first class.

All this was—had to be—ancillary to what he was doing. He was forced to depend on them: his attention was on the job. The anaesthetic was looking fine. All he knew was that he had what he needed and the woman's heart rate was great.

If only the baby's heartbeat held…

This was the moment of truth. He looked up to ask, but once again his needs were anticipated. The second of the older women stepped forward to push down on the uterus, giving him leverage as he slid one gloved hand into the incision.

Please…

'Here it comes.' He lifted the baby's head, turning it to the side to prevent it sucking in fluid. 'Yes!'

It was a perfect little girl.

Joss had only seconds to see that she was fine—the seconds while he scooped the baby free. As soon as she was free of her mother—before he'd even tied off the cord—hands were reaching for her, the sucker was in her mouth and they were removing mucus and freeing her to breathe. These people knew what they were doing! The old man behind Marie ducked in to scoop the infant into the waiting blanket as the elderly nurse cleared her airway.

23

'We'll be fine with her.' Amy motioned him back to the wound. 'She's looking good.'

He had no time to spare for the baby. He turned back to deliver the placenta, to swab and clamp and sew, hoping his geriatric helpers were able to clear the baby's airway in time.

Amy would supervise. He knew by now that she was a brilliant theatre nurse. She was acting as a competent anaesthetist. Apart from a couple of minor queries about dosage, he'd rarely had to intervene.

And as he began the lengthy repair process to the uterus there came the sound he'd been hoping for. The thin, indignant wail of a healthy baby.

The flattening of its heartbeat must have been stress-induced, he thought thankfully. A long labour and then the impact of the crash could have caused it.

How long had the girl been in labour?

A while, he thought, glancing to where Amy still monitored the intubator. The new mother was as white as death and the wound on her forehead still bled sluggishly. He'd suture it before she woke.

If she woke.

Why was she unconscious?

Hell, he needed technology. He needed to know if there was intracranial bleeding.

'We can do an ordinary X-ray here,' Amy said, and his eyes flew to hers. Once again she was thinking in front of him. 'We have the facilities. It won't show pressure if there's a build-up, but it'll show if there's a fracture.'

'Is there no way we can we get outside help?' He wanted a CT scan. He wanted his big city hospital—badly.

'Not until this rain eases.' Outside the window, the rain was still pelting down. 'Given decent conditions, a helicopter can land on the golf course, but not now. There's too many hills. The country's so rough that with visibility like this they'd be in real trouble.'

So they were still on their own.

'We'll be OK,' she said softly as he worked on. Their eyes locked and something passed between them. A bonding. They were in this together…

Joss felt a frown start behind his eyes. He didn't make contact like this with theatre staff. He didn't make contact with anyone. But this woman… It was as if she was somehow familiar…

She wasn't familiar at all. 'We're not finished yet. Let's get this abdominal cavity cleaned and stitched,' he said, more roughly than he'd intended, and bent back over his work.

Finally the job was done. Under Joss's guidance, Amy reversed the anaesthetic, concentrating fiercely every step of the way. At last, still rigid with anxiety, she removed the endotracheal tube and the woman took her first ragged breaths.

Amy had done it, and until now she hadn't known she could. She closed her eyes, and when she opened them again Joss was beside her, his hands on her shoulders and his face concerned.

'Are you OK?'

'I… Yes.' She tried to draw back but his eyes were holding her in place as firmly as his hands were holding her shoulders.

'Exactly how many anaesthetics have you given in your professional career?' he demanded, and she gave a rueful smile.

'Um…one,' she confessed. 'A tourist who had penile strangulation. The doctor from Bowra was here seeing someone else when he came in, screaming. I had no choice there either. If I hadn't given him the anaesthetic he'd have been impotent for life.'

'But…that's a really minor anaesthetic.'

'I know.' She took a deep breath. 'And, of course, as you reminded me, the insurance is a nightmare and if anything went wrong I could get sued for millions. So I shouldn't have done it, nor should I have done this one. But I've seen it done and, the way I figured, I didn't have a choice. Bleating to you about my lack of training wasn't going to help anything.'

She was amazing, he thought, stunned. Amazing!

'You were fantastic,' the woman called Marie said stoutly. 'To give an anaesthetic like that... She was wonderful, wasn't she, Doctor?'

Joss looked around at them all. He had four helpers in the room. Three geriatrics and Amy. And he had one live and healthy baby and one young woman whose colour was starting slowly to return to normal.

Because of these people, this baby would live and the unknown woman had been given a fighting chance. Because Amy had been prepared to take a chance, prepared to say to hell with the insurance risk, to hell with the legalities; because these old people had been prepared to shake off their retirement and do whatever they could, then this baby stood a chance of living. Living with a healthy mother.

'I think you're all wonderful,' he told them. He smiled at each of them in turn, but then his gaze returned to Amy's. And there was that jolt of...something. Something that he didn't recognise.

Whatever it was, it would have to wait. Now was not the time for questioning. 'I think you all deserve a medal,' he said softly. 'And I think we all deserve a happy ending. Which I think we'll get.'

He lifted the baby from Marie's arms and stood looking down at her. The tiny baby girl had wailed once, just to show she could, but she was now snuggled into the warmth of her prepared blanket and her creased eyes were blinking and gazing with wonder at this huge new world.

'You need your mum,' Joss said, and as if on cue there was a ragged gasp from the table. And another. Amy's eyes flew from the baby back to her patient.

'She's coming round,' she said softly. 'It needs only this to make it perfect.'

The woman was so confused she was almost incoherent, but she was definitely waking.

Joss took her hands, waiting with all the patience in the world for her to recover. When this woman had lost consciousness she'd been in a truck heading out of town. Now she was in hospital—kind of—and she was a mother. It would take some coming to terms with.

'You're fine,' he told her softly, his voice strong and sure, and Amy blinked to hear him. Joss looked decisive and tough but there was nothing tough about the way he spoke. He was gentleness itself. 'My name is Joss Braden. I'm a doctor and you're in hospital.' Of a sort. There was no need to go into details. 'Your truck crashed. You were in labour—remember?' And then at her weak nod, he smiled. 'You're not in labour any more. You've had a baby. The most gorgeous daughter.'

He held the child for her to see.

There was a long, long silence while she took that on board. Finally she seemed to manage it. She stared mutely at the softly wrapped bundle of perfect baby and then tears started trickling down her cheeks.

'Hey.' Joss was gentleness itself. One of his elderly nurses saw his need and handed him a tissue to dry her tears. 'There's not a lot to cry about. We're here to take care of you. We had to perform a Caesarean section but everything's fine.'

Her tears still flowed. Amy watched in silence, as did her three geriatric nurses.

There were more outside. The door was open—just a crack. How many ears were listening out there? Amy wondered and managed a smile. Well, why shouldn't they listen in to this happy ending? They'd worked as hard as she had, and they deserved it.

'Can you tell me your name?' Joss was saying.

'Charlotte…' It was a thready whisper.

'Charlotte who?'

Silence.

Her name could wait, Amy thought happily. Everything could wait now.

But Joss kept talking, assessing, concerned for the extent of damage to the young mother now that the baby had been delivered safely.

'Charlotte, you've had a head injury. I need to ask you a couple of questions, just so I'm sure you're not confused.'

She understood. Her eyes were still taking in her baby, soaking in the perfection of her tiny daughter, but she was listening to Joss.

'Do you know what the date is today?'

'Um…' She thought about it. 'Friday. Is it the twenty-fifth?'

'It sure is. Do you know who won the football grand final last week?'

That was easy. A trace of a smile appeared, and the girl shed years with it.

'The Bombers,' she said, and there was an attempt at flippancy. 'Hooray.'

'Hooray?' She was a brave girl. Amy grinned but Joss gave a theatrical groan.

'Oh, great. It's just my luck to bring another Bombers fan into the world.' Then he smiled and Amy, watching from the sidelines, thought, Wow! What a smile.

'And your surname?'

But that had been enough. The woman gave a tiny shake of her head and let her eyes close.

Joss nodded. He was satisfied. 'OK, Charlotte.' He laid a fleeting hand on the woman's cheek. 'We'll take some X-rays just to make sure there's no damage, then we'll let you and your daughter sleep.'

'So is anyone going to tell me what the set-up is here?'

With the young mother tucked up in a private room, her

baby by her side and no fewer than two self-declared inten-sive-care nurses on watch by her side, there was time for Amy and Joss to catch their breath.

'What would you like to know?' Amy was bone weary. She felt like she'd run a marathon. She hauled her white coat from her shoulders, tossed it aside and turned to unfasten the strings of Joss's theatre gear. They'd only had the one theatre gown, so the rest of their makeshift team had had to make do with white coats.

But making do with white coats was the last thing on Joss's mind. 'Tell me how I got a theatre staff,' he said. 'It was a miracle.'

'No more than us finding a doctor. That was the miracle. Of all the people to run into…'

'Yeah, it was her lucky day.' He gave a rueful grin and Amy smiled back. He had his back to her while she undid his ties and she was catching his smile in the mirror. He had the loveliest smile, she thought. Wide and white and sort of…chuckly. Nice.

In fact the whole package looked nice.

And as for Joss…

He stooped and hauled off the cloth slippers from over his shoes and then rose, watching while Amy did the same. Underneath her medical uniform Amy Freye was some par-cel.

She was tall, maybe five-ten or so. Her tanned skin was flawless. Her grey eyes were calm and serene, set in a lovely face. Her hair was braided in a lovely long rope and he sud-denly had an almost irresistable urge to…

Hey. What was going on here?

Get things back to a professional footing.

'What's someone with your skills doing in a place like this?' he asked lightly, and then watched in surprise as her face shuttered closed. Hell, he hadn't meant to pry. He only wanted to know. 'I mean… I assumed with your skills…'

'I'd be better off in a city hospital? Just lucky I wasn't,' she retorted.

'We were lucky,' he said seriously. 'We definitely were. If you hadn't been here we would have lost the baby.'

'You don't think Marie could have given the anaesthetic?'

'Now, that is something I don't understand.'

'Marie?'

'And her friends. Yes.'

She smiled then, and there were lights behind her grey eyes that were almost magnetic in their appeal. Her smile made a man sort of want to smile back. 'You like my team?'

'It's...different.'

She laughed, a lovely low chuckle. 'Different is right. An hour ago I was staring into space thinking, How on earth am I going to cope? I needed an emergency team, and I had no one. I thought, This place has no one but retirees. But retirees are people, too, and the health profession's huge. So I said hands up those with medical skills and suddenly I had an ambulance driver, two orderlies and three trained nurses. I've even got a doctor in residence, but he's ninety-eight and thinks he's Charles the First so we were holding him in reserve.'

She was fantastic. He grinned at her in delight.

This felt great, he thought suddenly. He'd forgotten medicine could feel like this. Back in Sydney he was part of a huge, impersonal team. His skills made him a troubleshooter, which meant that he was called in when other doctors needed help. He saw little of patients before they were on the operating table.

His staff were hand-picked, cool and clinically professional. But here...

They'd saved a life—what a team!

'I wouldn't ask it of these people every day,' Amy told him, unaware of the route his thoughts were taking. 'Marie's had three heart pills this morning to hold her angina at bay. Very few of my people are up to independent living but in an emergency they shine through. And even though Marie's heart is thumping away like a sledgehammer, there's no way she's going for a quiet lie-down now. She's needed, and if she dies being needed, she won't begrudge it at all.'

It was great. The whole set-up was great, but something was still worrying him. 'Where are the rest of your trained staff?'

That set her back. 'What trained staff?'

'This is a nursing home. I assume you have more skilled nurses than yourself.'

'I have two other women with nursing qualifications. Mary and Sue-Ellen. They do a shift apiece. Eight hours each. The three of us are the entire nursing population of Iluka.'

He frowned, thinking it through and finding it unsatisfactory. 'You need more...'

'No. Only eight of our beds are deemed nursing-home beds. The rest are hostel, so as long as we have one trained nurse on duty we're OK.'

'And in emergencies?'

'I can't call the others in. It means I don't have anyone for tonight.'

'What about holidays?'

'I do sixteen hours if either of the others are on holidays,' she said, with what was an attempt at lightness. 'It keeps me off the streets.'

She was kidding! 'That's crazy. The whole set-up's impossible.'

'You try attracting medical staff to Iluka.' She gave a weary smile. 'You try attracting anyone under the age of sixty to Iluka. Both my nurses are in their fifties and are here because their husbands have retired. Kitty, my receptionist, moved here to be with her failing mother, my cleaning and kitchen staff are well past retirement age, and there's no one else.'

'The town is a nursing home all by itself.'

'As you say.' She shrugged, and there was a pain behind

her eyes that he didn't understand. 'But we manage. Look at today. Weren't my oldies wonderful?'

'Wonderful.' But his mind was on her worries, not on what had just happened.

'So the two looking after the baby…'

'Marie and Thelma, and they're their element. Both are trained nurses with years of experience. Thelma has early Alzheimer's but she was matron of a Sydney hospital until she retired and there are some things that are almost instinctive. Marie's with her, and her experience is in a bush nursing hospital. She's physically frail but mentally alert so together they'll care for the mother and baby as no one else could. And I'm here if they need me.'

Joss looked across at her calm grey eyes. *'I'm here if they need me.'* It was said as a matter of course.

How often was she needed?

What was her story?

'Don't look so worried.' Her smile was meant to be reassuring. 'If I didn't think they'd manage—and love every moment of it—I'd be in there, helping. I'm only a buzz away.' Her smile faded as his look of concern deepened. 'What's worrying you? Charlotte's showing no sign of brain damage. The baby looks great. All we need to do is find out who she is.'

'Now, that's something else I don't understand.' His frown deepened. 'Jeff says she's not a Iluka resident and no one here recognises her.'

'No.' It had surprised Amy that she hadn't recognised the girl. She knew everyone in Iluka.

When she'd thought about it she'd even figured out where Joss fitted in. David and Daisy Braden had been speaking of nothing but their wonderful surgeon-son's visit for weeks. The whole town had known his exact arrival time, what Daisy was going to cook for him every night, where David intended to take him fishing and…

'What?' Joss asked, and Amy's lovely smile caused a dimple to appear right on the corner of her mouth.

It made him need to struggle hard to concentrate on what she was saying.

'Sorry. I was just thinking we should set the town onto finding out about our mystery mother. They told me all about you.'

'Did they?' He was disconcerted. He was trying really hard not to look at the dimple.

The observations that were happening were mutual. He looked nice when he was disconcerted, Amy decided.

Nice.

There was that word again but it described him absolutely. The more she saw of him the more she liked what she saw. Joss was taller than she was by a couple of inches. He had deep brown hair, curly, a bit sun-bleached and casually styled. His skin was bronzed and he had smiling green eyes.

And his clothes... He'd hauled off his sweater before they'd gone into Theatre but she'd been too rushed to notice, and then he'd put on a theatre gown. Now she was seeing his clothes for the first time.

They were...unexpected, to say the least. He was wearing faded, hip-hugging jeans and a bright white T-shirt with a black motif. The motif said:

'You've been a bad, bad girl. Go straight to my room.'

She blinked and blinked again. Then she grinned. This wasn't her standard image of a successful young surgeon. It was a rude, crude T-shirt. It shouldn't make her lips twitch.

'What?' he demanded, and her smile widened.

'I was thinking I shouldn't be in the same room as you—with that on.' She motioned to his T-shirt.

Damn. He'd forgotten he was wearing it. His father had given it to him for his birthday... Good old Dad, still trying to get his son moving in the wife department...

Fat chance.

But Amy had moved on. 'I need to talk to Jeff,' she said, and crossed to the door.

Joss frowned. 'I need to find him, too. He's looking after my dog. Or did one of your residents take him?'

'Lionel has him.' Her eyes creased into the smile he was starting to recognise. 'I saw him. Actually, I've heard about him, too. I thought he was much larger than he really is.'

'Have you been talking to my stepmother?'

Amy assumed an air of innocence. 'I might have been.'

He sighed. 'According to Daisy, he's the size of an elephant. That's because Bertram takes exception to anyone else sitting on my knee—and her dratted Peke decided it would grace me with its favours.'

'Lucky you.'

'As you say.' He shook off the light-headedness he was feeling. Was it the crash? Or…was it just the way she made him feel? Like he ought to get the conversation back to medicine—fast.

'Sergeant Packer and I could find no sign of identification at all in the mother's truck. But he is able to run a plate check. We're hoping we can find out who she is that way.'

She nodded. 'And I guess we need to fully examine the baby.'

'I'll do that now.'

'Thank you.'

Joss nodded, aware that he was retreating. He'd come out of his shell a little—a very little—but he didn't want to stay out.

He had to leave.

'I'm going to have to figure out how I can get away from this place,' he said.

Her brows rose at that. 'You're leaving?'

'I was. Until my car was totalled.'

'Your father said you were here for two weeks.'

'Yeah, well…'

'The honeymoon couple were a bit much for you, were

they?' Her eyes danced in sympathy, demanding that he smile in return.

'You know my father and Daisy?'

'I certainly do.' She grinned. 'Until she met your father, Daisy had her name down here as a potential resident.'

'Oh, yeah.' Right.

'They're very happy,' she said—and waited.

And out it came. 'They're always happy.'

'Excuse me?'

'My father's been married four times.' It was impossible to keep the bitterness from his voice.

She thought about that. Looking at his face, she saw the layers of pain behind the bald fact.

'Divorce?'

'Death. Every time.'

That made it so much worse. 'I'm sorry.'

'Yeah.' He gave a laugh that came out harsher than he'd intended. 'You'd think he'd learn.'

'That people die?'

'Yes.'

'You can be unlucky,' Amy said softly. 'Or you can be lucky. I guess your dad has had rotten luck.'

'He keeps trying to replace…'

'Your mother?'

He caught himself. What was he saying? He was talking as if she was really interested. As if he wanted to share…

She was a nurse. A medical colleague. He didn't get close to medical colleagues.

He didn't get close to anyone.

But she'd seen the expression on his face. She knew he needed to move on.

'But you *do* have two weeks' holiday, right?' she probed. 'Being stuck here isn't a disaster.'

'I'll get out.'

'How?'

That stymied him. 'I guess…when it stops raining…'

'If it stops raining.'

'There's no need to sound like a prophet of doom,' he snapped. 'It'll rain for forty days and forty nights so collect your cats and dogs and unicorns and build a boat…'

She chuckled. 'OK. *When* it stops raining. But it'll take some time to get the bridge repaired. Maybe we can get a ferry working.'

'I could get out by helicopter.' But he sounded dubious and for good reason.

'Even when it stops raining I doubt you'll persuade one to land here unless it's an emergency. Being weary of watching your father and his new wife cuddle each other might not fit into the category of emergency.'

'The sea…'

'Have you seen the harbour? There's no way a boat's putting to sea until this weather dies.' She shrugged. 'Sure, there are boats which will bring supplies when the weather backs off but until then… I'm afraid you're stuck with us, Joss.'

He liked the way she said his name, he decided. It was sort of lilting. Different.

But he had more important things to think of than lilting voices. His own voice took on a hint of desperation. 'I can't go back to stay with Dad and Daisy. I'm going around the twist!'

'That bad?'

'They hold hands. *Over the breakfast table!*'

Amy choked on laughter. 'So you're not a romantic, Dr Braden. Well, I never. And you with that T-shirt.'

He had the grace to grin. 'OK. Despite the T-shirt, I'm not a romantic. Is there a hotel in town?'

'Nope.'

Sigh. 'I don't suppose there's a room available here.'

'You don't suppose your father would be mortally offended if you stayed in a nursing home rather than with him?'

He would. Damn.

But she was thinking for him. 'What excuse did you give—when you left so suddenly?'

'That I had to prepare a talk for a conference. It was worrying me so I thought I'd get back early to Sydney to do some preparation.' Then, at her look, Joss gave an exasperated sigh. 'It's the truth. I do.'

'I believe you.' Another chuckle. 'Though thousands wouldn't. But you've solved your own problem.'

'I have?'

She hesitated, and then said slowly, as if she wasn't sure she was doing the right thing but wanted to anyway, 'If you need privacy then maybe you can stay at my place. It's a great isolated spot for writing conference material.'

'Don't you live here?'

'Are you kidding?' She smiled, and he thought suddenly she shed years when she smiled. She really was extraordinarily lovely. 'Give me a break. I'm twenty-eight years old. I'm not quite ready to live in a retirement home full time.'

Twenty-eight... What was a twenty-eight-year-old incredibly skilled theatre nurse doing in a place like Iluka?

Caring for a husband? For parents? Unconsciously he found his eyes drifting to the third finger of her left hand. Which was tucked in the folds of her dress. Damn.

'Um...so where do you live?'

'Millionaire's Row.'

'Pardon?'

'Didn't your father show you round the town?'

'Yes...' He thought back and then his eyes widened. 'Don't tell me you live in one of *those*.'

There could be no mistaking his meaning. Amy chuckled again and shrugged. 'Of course. I live in the biggest and the most ostentatious mansion of them all, and I do so all on my lonesome. I have nine spare bedrooms and three whole spas you can choose from. You can have one and your dog another. You can tell your father that you need to be alone to write—and you can be. You can sit and write conference notes to your heart's content and we need never see each other. If that's what you want.'

Of course it was what he wanted. Wasn't it? But…that smile…

Damn, there was so much here that he didn't understand.

'Tell you what,' she said. 'I have heaps to do and you have a baby and a dog to check, and maybe you need to see Sergeant Packer about your car—or what's left of it. Lunch is at twelve and you're very welcome to eat with us. I'm off at two. If you can keep yourself amused until then, I'll take you home.'

'You make me sound like a stray puppy,' he complained, and her smile widened.

'That's how you sound.'

'Hey…'

Her grey eyes twinkled. 'I know. Nurse subordination to doctors has never been my strong point. Dreadful, isn't it? Are you sure you don't want to reconsider?'

But Joss was sure. He definitely didn't want to spend any more time with his father and Daisy.

And the more he saw of Amy Freye, the more he thought a few days in the same house wouldn't be such a bad idea.

Was he mad? What on earth was he thinking?

'Um…no, I won't reconsider,' he told her, and she laughed. It was as if she knew what he was thinking, and the feeling was distinctly disconcerting.

'Until two o'clock,' she told him—and left him to make of her what he would.

CHAPTER THREE

THE house was stunning.

Amy drove Joss and Bertram out to Millionaire's Row and turned her car off the road into a driveway leading to a mansion. As she had said, it was the most ostentatious house on Millionaire's Row. Which left him more confused than ever. Amy's car looked as if her next date was with the wrecker. Her dress was faded and shabby. She looked as if she hadn't a penny to bless herself with, yet the house she lived in was extraordinary.

Or maybe extraordinary was an understatement.

It was set back from the beach but it had maybe a quarter of a mile of beachfront all of its own. The house was two storeys high and huge. It was built of something like white marble and the entire edifice glistened in the rain like some sort of miniature palace.

Or maybe not so miniature…

'Wow,' he said, stunned, and Amy looked across at him and smiled.

'Welcome to my humble abode.' Her smile was mocking.

'It's…'

'Ostentatious? Over the top? Don't I know it.' She pulled into one bay of what appeared to be an eight- or ten-car garage and switched off the engine. The car spluttered to a halt, and a puff of black smoke spat out from under the bonnet.

'Um…about your priorities…'

'Yes?'

'You don't think you might do with one bedroom less and get yourself a new car?'

She appeared offended. 'What's wrong with my car?'

'Er…nothing.' He hesitated and then decided on honesty. 'Well, actually—everything.'

'Bertram likes it.' She swung herself out of the car and opened the rear door for Bertram. She ran a hand under the silky velvet of his ears as he nosed his way out of his comfortable back seat, and the big dog shivered with pleasure. Amy grinned. 'If your dog likes it, who are you to quibble? He's a gentleman of taste if ever I saw one.'

Joss smiled in return. Her grin was infectious. Gorgeous! 'Bertram likes smells and there'd be enough smells in your car to last a dog a lifetime. I reckon there are four or five generations of smells in that back seat.'

But she wasn't listening to criticisms of her ancient car. She was intent on Bertram's wonderful ears. 'He's lovely.'

'You don't have ten dogs of your own?'

'No.' Her voice clipped off short at that, as if collecting herself, and Joss gave her a strange look. There were so many things here that he didn't understand.

'Come through.' She flicked a switch and the garage doors slid shut behind them, and then she walked up the wide steps into the house. 'Welcome to my world.'

It grew more astonishing by the minute.

The house was vast but it contained barely a scrap of furniture. Joss walked through a wide passage leading to room after room, and each door led to a barren space. 'What the…?'

'I only live in the back section of the house,' she told him over her shoulder as she walked. 'Don't worry. There's a spare bed.'

He was staring around him and he was stunned. 'You own this whole house?'

'Sort of.' She was leading the way into a vast kitchen-living area. Here was a simple table and two chairs, two armchairs which had seen better days and a television set. Black and white. Nothing else.

It grew curiouser and curiouser. *He* grew curiouser and curiouser.

'You'll have to explain.'

'Why?'

Why? Of course she didn't need to explain anything. He was her guest. She was doing him a favour by putting him up. But...

'I'm intrigued,' he admitted, and she grinned.

'Good. I like my men intrigued.'

He was more intrigued by the minute, he thought faintly. She was a total enigma. And when she smiled... Whew!

'Will you tell me?'

'It's a long story.'

'By the look of the weather I have forty days and forty nights to listen.'

'I need to go back to work.'

'I thought you were off duty.'

'I have paperwork to do, and I don't want to leave our new mother for too long. Mary's there now but I don't like to leave her on her own. I'll stay for an hour but...'

'Then we have an hour. Tell me.'

Amy made a cup of tea first. Hell, she really did have nothing, he thought as he watched her spoon tea leaves into a battered teapot and pour the tea into two chipped mugs. Nothing.

Poor little rich girl...

'This house was my stepfather's,' she told him.

Joss took his mug of tea and sat, and Bertram flopped down beside him. It seemed almost ridiculous to sit in this vast room. Somewhere there should be a closet where this furniture should fit.

It wouldn't need to be a very big closet.

'Was?'

She sank into the opposite chair and by the look on her face he knew she was very glad to sit. Once more there was the impression of exhaustion. She looked like someone who had driven herself hard, for a very long time.

'Was?' he said again, and she nodded.

'Yes.'

'And now?'

'It's mine—on the condition that I live in it for ten years.'

He stared around in distaste. 'He didn't leave you any furniture?'

'No.'

'Then…' He hesitated. 'You haven't thought of maybe selling the place and buying something smaller?'

'Didn't you listen? I said I had to live in it for ten years.'

He thought that over. 'So you're broke.'

'Yes. Absolutely. It costs a fortune to keep this place.'

'Maybe you could take in lodgers.'

'Lodgers don't come to live in Iluka.' She hesitated and then sighed. She sat leaning forward, cradling her mug as if she was gaining warmth from its contents. As indeed she was. The house was damp and chill. It needed heating…

'Don't even think about it,' Amy told him, seeing where he was looking. The central-heating panels almost mocked them. 'Have you any idea of what it costs to heat this place?'

'Why don't lodgers come to live in Iluka?'

'The same reason no one comes to live in Iluka. Except for retirees.'

'You'll have to explain.'

'The town has nothing.'

'Now, that's something else I don't understand,' he complained. 'My father's married Daisy and seems delighted with the idea of coming to live here. There's a solid residential population…'

'On half-acre blocks which are zoned residential. We have a general store, a post office and nothing else. No one else has ever been allowed to build here.'

'Why?'

'My stepfather owned the whole bluff and he put caveats on everything.'

'So?'

'So there's no land under half an acre available for sale. Ever. That means this strip along the beach has been bought by millionaires and it's used at peak holiday times. The rest has been bought by retirees living their rural dream. But for many it's turned into a nightmare.'

'How so?'

'There's nothing here.' She spread her hands. 'People come here and see the dream—golf courses, bowling clubs, miles and miles of golden beaches—so they buy and they build. But then they discover they need other services. Medical services. Entertainment. Shops. And there's nothing. There's no school so there's no young population. No land's ever been allocated for commercial premises. There's just nothing. So couples retire here for the dream and when one of them gets sick…' She hesitated. 'Well, until I built the nursing home it was a disaster. It meant they had to move on.'

'That's something else I don't understand,' he complained. 'You built the nursing home? How did you do that when you can't even afford a decent teacup?'

Amy rose and crossed to a kitchen drawer, found what she was looking for and handed it over.

He read in silence. 'To my stepdaughter, Amy Freye, I leave my home, White-Breakers.

'I also leave her the land on Shipwreck Bluff and sufficient funds to build a forty-bed nursing home…'

He read to the end, confusion mounting. Then he laid it aside and looked up to find her watching him.

'Now do you see?'

'I do—sort of.'

'This place was desperate for a nursing home. There's been huge numbers of couples for whom it's been a tragedy in the past, couples where one has ended up in a nursing home in Bowra because they were too frail to cope at home but the other was stuck here until the end. And each time, as isolation and helplessness set in, my stepfather would offer to buy them out of their property for far less than they'd paid. He did it over and over. He found it a real little gold mine.'

He was struggling to understand. 'Surely they didn't have to sell their properties back to him. Surely they could have sold on the open market?'

'With the restrictions on the place? No. It's better now, but then... Then it was impossible.'

'So where do you fit in?'

'I don't.'

That made Joss raise his eyebrows. 'I beg your pardon?'

'My stepfather and I...didn't get on.'

'Why doesn't that surprise me?'

Amy gave a mirthless laugh, then stooped to give Bertram a hug. Like she needed to hug someone. Something.

She hadn't had enough hugs in her life, Joss thought with sudden insight and he put a hand out as if to touch her...

It was an instinctive reaction and it didn't make sense. She looked at his hand, surprised, and he finally drew it away. It was as if he'd surprised himself. Which he had.

'So tell me why he's left you this—and tell me why you're in trouble.'

She blinked and blinked again. The concern in his voice was enough to shake her foundations.

No one was concerned for her. No one. Not even Malcolm.

'I...I need to get back.'

'No.' He stood and lifted the mug from her hands, placed it on the sink and then put his hands on her shoulders. Gently he pressed her into the opposite chair, then sat down himself. His eyes didn't leave hers. They were probing and caring and kind—and she felt tears catch behind her eyes. Damn, she never cried. It must be the pressure and the emotions of the morning, she thought. Or...something.

But Joss was still watching her. Waiting.

'I… It's just… I'm fine. The terms of the will…'

'Are draconian.'

'I guess.' She shook her head. 'You have no idea.'

'So tell me.'

She shrugged and then settled in for the long haul. 'My mother married my stepfather when I was nine years old. We came here. But we soon learned that my stepfather was a control freak. He was…appalling. My mother's health was precarious at the best of times. He bullied her, he manipulated her—and he hated me.'

'Because you were feisty?'

'Feisty?' Amy looked startled and then gave a reluctant chuckle. 'Well, maybe I was. I only know that my own father had taught me that the world was my oyster, and here was my stepfather drilling into me that I was only a girl, and I wasn't even to be educated because that was such a waste. There wasn't a school here so I had to do my lessons by correspondence but he took delight in interrupting. In controlling, controlling, controlling.'

Joss thought it through—to the obvious, but dreadful next step. He thought about it for a moment and then decided, hell, he'd risk it. In his years as a doctor he'd learned it was better to confront the worst-case scenario head on. So he asked.

'He didn't abuse you?'

That shocked her out of her introspection. She took a deep breath and shook her head. She might be shocked by the bluntness of his question, but the idea wasn't incredible. 'No,' she told him. 'Apart from hitting me—which he did a lot—he didn't touch me. But…' She shuddered then, as if confessing something that had been hidden for a very long time. 'The awful thing is that it's not such a stupid question. I'm sure he wanted to. The way he looked at me. It was only…that was the only matter in which my mother stood up to him. If he ever touched me—like that—she'd have gone straight to the police, she told him, and she meant it. So he hated me from a distance. Oh, he hated me.'

'So you left?'

'As soon as I was fifteen I was out of here. Somehow I ended up in a city refuge, I met some great people and I managed to get myself educated. There's help if homeless kids want it badly enough. Which I did. I would have liked to have done medicine but that was impossible so I made it nursing. But my mother…she wasn't allowed to contact me, and she was getting worse. Medically there was nothing here for her. So my mother and many more of the population here were being screwed by my stepfather for everything they had, and there wasn't a thing I could do about it. I wasn't allowed home unless I promised I'd give up nursing and stay here permanently.'

'The man was a megalomaniac,' he said, stunned, and she nodded.

'He was.' She shrugged. 'Maybe I should have come home but I didn't know—couldn't guess—how ill my mother was. When my mother died I was so angry… But at least, or so I thought, I'd never have to have anything more to do with my stepfather. But my independence still rankled. It must have, because when he died he left this crazy will.'

'Leaving you the lot.' Joss frowned. 'Maybe because he felt sorry for the way he treated you.'

'No.' Anger flashed out then. 'Not because he felt sorry for me. No way. It was a last gesture to get at me. He knew I'd come. Because of my mother's distress and because her friends here were in such trouble, he knew the idea of setting up a nursing home would be irresistible. But he and his nephews after him have made sure that I haven't a cent other than what was put into the terms of the will.'

'He's left you nothing else?'

'He's left barely enough to cover the running costs of the home—though we do get government subsidies now and it's improving. But still… I'm allowed to take out my nurse-manager salary and that's it. Even that often has to be ploughed back to make up shortfalls. The nephews removed the furniture—everything that wasn't nailed down. Their plan is to make me as uncomfortable as possible so I'll leave, because if I go before the ten years is up they'll have the lot.'

'And how many of your ten years have gone?'

'Four.'

'Six years to go?'

'Six years of purgatory,' she said—lightly, but he knew it was just that.

'Is there any relief?'

'I… Yes.' Amy sighed and then managed a smile. 'Oh, of course there is. Heck, in six years' time I'll be fabulously wealthy.'

'Is that why you're doing it?' Somehow he didn't think it could be, and her answer was no surprise.

'No.' Her response was fierce. 'I'd walk away if I could, but the covenants he's put on this place are unbelievable. People like your stepmother moved here in all faith but they found they've done their money cold. There's nothing here for them. The nursing home is their only hope for future support.'

'I don't understand.'

'Talk to the lawyers,' she said wearily. 'They'll tell you. The place is a disaster and if I walk away there'll be three or four hundred couples who'll have to walk away with me. They'll lose everything they own.'

'As bad as that?'

'As bad as that.'

Silence. Then: 'Do you have any support at all?'

She caught herself then. 'I… Of course I do. There's Malcolm.'

'Malcolm?'

'My fiancé.'

Her fiancé.

Of course. There had to be a fiancé. For the first time he concentrated on her hands and there it was, a diamond solitaire, declaring to the world that she was taken.

Well. That was fine. Wasn't it?

Of course it was. There was no reason in the world for his gut to wrench.

But she'd risen and was laying her coffee-mug on the sink, intent on the next thing. 'I need to go.'

'Yeah?'

'Yeah. I'll call you if I need you.'

'Did you come home just to offload me?' he asked, and she grinned.

'Of course. Why else would I come home in the middle of the day?'

'Because you're off duty?'

'There is that. But I have paperwork to do, and I really would like to be there for our new mum.'

'You'll ring me the minute you're worried?'

'The minute I'm worried I'll be here in my wreckage-mobile to cart you back to the hospital so fast you can't blink.'

'Wreckage-mobile permitting?'

'Wreckage-mobile permitting.'

'You realise if you leave then I'm stuck?'

Amy thought about that. 'Do you want me to drop you off at your father's?'

'No!'

'There you go, then.' She smiled. 'A willing captive. My very favourite sort.'

Humph.

Willing captive or not, as soon as she left that was how Joss did feel. Trapped.

He explored the house—sort of—but a proper tour could take days. He figured out which bedroom Amy used. That'd be the room with blankets on the single bed and one ancient and overflowing dresser.

Then he figured out his bedroom—the one with the single bedstead and nothing else—though surprisingly there were blankets and linen folded at the end. It seemed as if Amy did have guests.

Guest, he corrected himself. One guest and one guest only sometimes. Not often.

'So where's this Malcolm?' he asked, and was surprised to hear the note of anger in his voice.

But there were no answers.

Bertram was loping along by his side and he apologised in advance for the sleeping arrangements. 'This is a single bed,' he told his dog. 'That means me. On my own. No bed-sharing with you!'

The dog looked at him mournfully and Joss folded his ears back. In truth he liked the dog sleeping with him as much as Bertram liked obliging.

Sleeping by himself was the pits.

'Can you tell me where this fiancé comes in?' he asked of Bertram, and Bertram cocked a head to one side as if thinking about it. 'Yeah, like me, you don't understand. If he's such a hero, why doesn't he loan her some furniture? If she was my girl...'

Now that was not a thought worth pursuing.

Damn, what was he going to do with himself? Isolation was all very well, but...

He needed things. Like a razor. Like a spare shirt. He thought about his belongings. They'd been in the trunk of his car and the trunk had been mangled into the steering-wheel. Any razor would be matchsticks.

His laptop had been sitting on the floor of the front passenger seat. Maybe it was OK. Please...

He could ring the police sergeant and find out if anything was salvageable. Jeff would probably still be out at the wreck, clearing debris and making the roadblocks safe.

But he'd quite like to return to the hospital. Charlotte's head injury was a worry. In her condition, not to have a doctor on standby seemed downright dangerous.

There was only one solution.

Sighing, he lifted his phone from his belt and called his father.

'So tell me about Amy Freye.'

He was still sitting at Amy's kitchen table while his father and his father's new wife clucked their concern about his accident and stared around them with open-mouthed astonishment. It seemed they'd never been in Amy's home and they were stunned. 'No, Daisy, I don't want another cup of tea. I want some gossip.'

But he wouldn't get gossip from this pair. He'd get nothing but praise.

'Amy's wonderful,' Daisy declared. 'She's saved this town single-handed.'

'Explain.'

And he got the story again—the same story Amy had told him, embellished with gratitude.

'The old man robbed us blind,' Daisy told him, easy tears appearing in her eyes at the memory. 'We—my late husband and I—moved here because we were stupid, and as soon as we bought we were stuck fast. Oh, we thought it was fantastic when we first arrived but then John got sick and there was nothing. Not even a pharmacy. I spent my life on the road between here and Bowra, and then when John got worse he had to go into the Bowra Nursing Home. I figured that I'd have to sell—but people had woken up by then that there was never going to be any commercial development.'

'No commercial development at all?'

'No.' She sighed and shook her head. 'There's one general store and a post office—that's it. During the height of the season there's supplies from Sydney delivered to the millionaires, but that style of shopping is out of the range of ordinary people like us. The wealthy like their isolation but for us…it's the pits. So I was stuck. I couldn't get a buyer at half the price we paid. Then John died. And fortunately so did Amy's stepfather. Then Amy arrived and it's all different.'

'How is it different?'

'Every way you can think of,' Daisy said roundly. 'She's built the home but she's done so much more. She runs meals on wheels to take decent dinners to the old folk stuck at home. She runs shopping rosters so we're not always in the car to Bowra. The nursing home's set up so the Bowra doctor can visit and do minor procedures here. She's organised pharmacy supplies so we can get urgent medicine. Everything. Half the people in Iluka are still in their homes today because of Amy.'

'I could never have moved here without her,' his father told him. 'I met Daisy when I came to play an interclub bowls match and it felt like heaven. But then Daisy told me the problems she's been having… We still couldn't sell her place, but with Amy we're safe for another six years.'

'For as long as she's stuck here,' Joss said thoughtfully.

'Yes. And even after that. As long as she puts up with us for the legal ten years, then the nursing home will be a going concern for ever.'

'There's a lot riding on her staying.'

'She has a good heart,' Daisy said roundly. 'She'll stay.'

'And she's engaged to a local man.'

'Sort of. Malcolm is an accountant in Bowra and his dad's a lawyer. He met Amy when his father was looking after Amy's legal affairs and…well, there's a bit of a dearth of young men around here.'

'He doesn't look after her very well.'

'Well, they're not married.'

'If I was engaged to Amy…'

'Yes, dear, but you're not,' Daisy said patiently. 'And, of course, Malcolm can't move here. His practice is in Bowra and when it rains it floods and the road's cut. Though not always as spectacularly as it is now.'

There was a lot he still didn't understand but it was time to move on.

'You guys have two cars, right?'

His father and stepmother looked at each other. 'Yes, but…'

He saw where their thoughts were headed. 'No, I'm not planning to try a stunt jump over the river. I know I'm stuck here.'

'You're very welcome to stay with us for as long as you like,' Daisy told him, and his father beamed his consent. They'd come out to Amy's practically twittering with excitement, and now they were aching to take him home.

'I'm happy here,' he told them, and Daisy looked around and shuddered.

'Yes, dear, but it's hardly cosy.'

'And that's something else I wanted to talk to you about. Look at this place.'

They looked—and they could only agree.

'We didn't think she lived like this,' Daisy told him. She was clearly puzzled. 'We thought…well, she lives in such a huge house we thought that her clothes and her car were a sort of eccentric choice.'

'She has no money.'

His parents looked shocked at the thought. 'Of course she has money. She lives in this place…'

'Which is costing her a bomb, but she can't even afford to heat it. I gather she has no money at all.'

'She told you that?'

'Yes.'

'But you've only just met her.'

'I have a very confiding nature,' Joss told them, and got an odd look from his stepmother for his pains.

'She really has nothing?'

'So I gather. The old man left everything but the house and the nursing home to his nephews.'

They practically gaped. And then Daisy moved straight into the organisational mode Joss was starting to dread. 'Well! I'm sure we could find all sorts of furniture to give her and so could half the population of Iluka. If we'd had any idea... Most of us are in a position to give. We think so much of Amy...'

'It wouldn't work.' Joss was doing some on-the-spot thinking. 'She'd sell it. She's strapped for cash and the nephews are breathing down her neck for more. But if you lent her things...'

'Lent?'

'Like, for six years. Would you do that?'

He watched their faces and saw the measure of respect and affection in which Amy was held. There was no hesitation at all. 'Of course we would.'

'We'll get onto this straight away,' his father told him. 'It'll be a pleasure to do it. If the town had known... I know Jack Trotter—he's Shire President. I'm sure there's things we can do. This town's coffers are very healthy indeed—there's not a lot of traffic lights that need maintaining around here. Come to think of it, there's not a lot of anything that needs maintaining. Now, how about you, lad? You don't want to stay here, I assume?' He looked around the barren room in distaste. 'It puts a man off money, seeing the place like this.'

'It does.' But Joss hesitated. 'If it's all the same to you, Dad, I might stay on. If you can lend me one of your cars...'

'Surely.' But his father's face was a question. 'But why?'

'It's just... The reason I was leaving was to get down to work on this conference paper. That still applies. This place is quiet...'

'And you need to be here as our furniture arrives.' Daisy was smiling in a way Joss didn't like. It meant his stepmother was reading far too much into his intention to stay. 'You leave the boy be, David. He doesn't want to be staying with a couple of oldies like us when he could be staying with Amy.'

'Amy's engaged,' David said, surprised. He'd caught the gist of where Daisy was headed but he didn't follow.

'Yes, she is,' Daisy muttered, and Joss raised his eyebrows.

'You don't like this Malcolm?'

'No.' Daisy was blunt and decisive.

'That's not really fair.' Joss's father was frowning. 'You hardly know the man.'

'I know that he's wishy-washy.'

'He's a decent bloke.'

'He's never going to set the world on fire,' Daisy retorted. 'He's an accountant in Bowra and he's the sort of man you'd know from five years old that was where he'd end up.'

'That's a bit harsh. Amy must like him,' Joss said mildly, and Daisy snorted.

'Yeah. Like she had a choice. He's a presentable young man and presentable young men are a bit thin on the ground here. And as for Malcolm… He's onto a very good thing with Amy Freye and he's enough of a money manager to know it.'

'In six years, maybe.'

'Would you take great trouble to hold onto a gold mine even though you knew it wouldn't pay out for six years?'

He thought that through. 'I guess I would.'

'There you go, then,' Daisy said triumphantly. 'He's wishy-washy and a gold-digger. I rest my case.'

CHAPTER FOUR

Joss returned to the hospital to find Charlotte was sleeping. Amy was taking her obs as he walked into her room. She had her white coat on over her clothes again and he thought again how strikingly attractive she was. Once she was out of those dreary clothes...

Maybe he could get Daisy onto that, too.

But Amy was smiling and he thought, Why bother? She was gorgeous enough as she was.

Luckily, Amy wasn't into mind-reading. She was concentrating on her patient. 'She's hardly stirred.'

'She's due for some pain relief.' He took the chart and wrote up what was needed—and then he hesitated. 'I suppose we have the necessary drugs...'

'Because we're isolated I have permission to run a limited pharmacy. I have what's needed.'

He shook his head in appreciation. 'This is an amazing nursing home.'

'It is,' she said without any false modesty. 'But didn't I have you trapped at home?'

'My father and Daisy came to the rescue. I am currently driving Daisy's pink Volkswagen.'

She grinned. 'I bet your dad's relieved. He might be in love but even he blanched when she had it spray-painted pink.'

'Bertram took one look and elected to stay at home.'

'Wise dog.'

'But I thought I might be needed here.'

'So you decided to brave even a pink Volkswagen. What a man!'

She was laughing at him. He liked it, he decided. He definitely liked it.

'Maybe I'm not needed,' he said, moving on but not without a struggle. 'Things are looking good here. The baby's still fine?'

'Yep. She's in the sitting room with the oldies. My nursing staff decided that while her mother slept they could babysit.'

'So we have…twenty babysitters?'

'At least. Charlotte will be lucky if she gets her daughter back. Talk about a case of collective cluck.'

'I wonder who she is.'

'I wonder.' Amy followed his gaze to the sleeping mother. 'She looks exhausted.'

'But she's not a local?'

'I'd reckon every single one of our residents managed to get a look at her on the way in and no one recognises her.'

'Her truck looks like a farm truck.'

'And that's what she looks like. A farmer. Her hands…they're work hands.' She lifted the girl's fingers gently from the counterpane. Joss saw and thought that they had matching hands. The stranger's hands were work-worn but so were Amy's. Both women knew how to work hard.

'She'll tell us soon enough when she wakes.'

'I'm not sure.' Amy was still watching the girl's face. 'She woke for a little but she seems…she seems almost afraid.'

'There's nothing to be afraid of here.'

'Apart from being cosseted to death. What a place to have a baby. There are no fewer than five sets of bootees and matinée jackets being knitted as we speak.'

'Fate worse than death.'

'As you say.'

They left Charlotte sleeping and made their way to Amy's office. Charlotte was nicely stable and the baby was doing beautifully. There was no reason for him to stay, but Joss made no move to leave.

There wasn't a good reason for him to leave, Amy figured, remembering where he was going home to. So she might as well make use of the man.

'How do you feel about checking Rhonda Coutts's lungs?'

'Rhonda Coutts?'

'I think she might be building up to pneumonia. She had a fall last week and spent a few days on her back. She's up now but she's coughing and she's weak. As the Bowra doctor can't get through...well, would you check her?'

'Sure.' Rhonda Coutts's lungs. Well, well.

He was a surgeon—one of the top in his field. It had been a long time since he'd been called on to advise about the possible pneumonia of an elderly patient with no surgical background.

She sensed his hesitation. 'Would you feel competent...?'

He bristled. 'Hey, of course I'm competent.'

'I only thought...well, with you being a surgeon you might have...'

'Forgotten?'

'I'm sorry.' She gave a rueful smile. 'Insulting, huh?'

'No. It's fine.' He was still bristling. 'Lead the way to Mrs Coutts.'

'I have a real live doctor on tap. For a week, if I'm lucky. What I won't be able to achieve in a week...'

Kitty, Amy's secretary, was staring at her as if she was demented as Amy danced in to fetch Mrs Coutts's medical records. 'What on earth are you talking about?'

But Amy was practically whooping on the spot as she planned ahead. 'Mr Harris's ingrown toenails. Ethel Crane's eczema. Martin Hamilton's prostate. They can all be seen here. Now.'

Martin's prostate was the best one. The Bowra doctor was

a middle-aged woman and Martin wouldn't consent to speaking to her about his prostate, much less let her examine him. 'With a doctor right here, I can solve all these problems in one fell swoop.'

'But he's here on holiday,' Kitty said doubtfully. 'Do you think he will?'

'He's staying at my house.' Amy's jubilation faded a little when she thought of that—she'd felt embarrassed to ask him out to the shambles that was her home but the upside was that it put him nicely in her debt. 'And he's proud, Kitty. I only have to suggest to the man that he can't and he will. The man's a renowned surgeon after all, and he's a walking ego if ever I saw one, so I don't see why we can't use him.'

'He seems…nice.' Kitty was still doubtful.

'He's a man, isn't he?' Amy demanded. 'Therefore he's here to be used. And use him I will, for however long I have.'

All the signs were that Mrs Coutts did have pneumonia and as Joss put away his stethoscope she burst into tears.

'I'm not going to hospital,' she sobbed. 'I should never have let you examine me. I'm not leaving here.'

'You have the odds in your favour,' Amy said wryly. She sat on the bed and took the elderly lady's hands in hers. 'Rhonda, remember the bridge?'

Her sobs arrested as the old lady looked up at Amy—and then burst into tears again.

'But I'll die. If I can't go to hospital…'

Amy gave Joss a rueful grin and hugged the old lady. 'You know, there is a third choice.' As Rhonda sobbed on, Amy put her away from her and forced her wrinkled face up so her eyes met her own. 'Rhonda, look who we've got. Our very own doctor, for however long the rain takes to subside. We have a really extensive drug cupboard—all the supplies we need we have right here—and you have your own personal physician.'

Rhonda stared. She hiccuped on a sob, then sniffed and looked up at Joss.

'He's as stuck as we are,' Amy told her, and grinned.

And finally Rhonda smiled.

'Really?'

'You'll look after Rhonda, won't you, Dr Braden?' Amy asked submissively, but there was nothing submissive in her twinkle as she looked up at him.

And there was no choice.

'Yes,' he said, goaded, but then he looked at the old lady in the bed and thought, Damn, they were all in this together. They were all stuck. And he was sure the X-ray he intended to take would verify she had pneumonia.

'Of course I will,' he said in a voice that was much more gentle. 'How can you doubt it?'

After that he saw Mr Harris's ingrown toenails, Ethel Crane's eczema, Martin Hamilton's prostate and Kitty's splinter under her thumbnail just for good measure.

'I've been meaning to do something about it for a few days but it's such a hassle to go to Bowra,' the secretary told him, blushing as he held her hand and gently examined her inflamed finger. 'And now Amy says you're here to be used... I mean she says you don't mind being doctor...'

Joss caught Amy's eye—and there was laughter there! She looked like a child caught out in mischief.

She was enchanting, he thought. Enchanting! The more he saw of her the more she had him fascinated.

She was using him for all she was worth.

But even her effrontery had its limits. She helped administer a local anaesthetic to Kitty's thumb, then watched as he cut a tiny section out of the nail to remove the splinter—he really was an excellent operator, she thought with satisfaction—and then she decided it was time he was dismissed. After all, he'd had a rough day—and she had plans for him in the morning.

'Maybe it's time you finished for the day,' she told him. 'You've been very useful.'

'Gee, thanks.'

'Think nothing of it.' She glanced at her watch. 'There's not much to eat at home but if you don't want to eat with your parents maybe you could grab yourself something from the general store. They're open until six so you have half an hour.'

Wow, that sounded exciting. He didn't think.

'And you?'

'I'll eat here.' It didn't cost her to eat at the hospital—but she wasn't admitting that.

'Do you need to stay here?' he demanded. By now he'd met Mary—Amy's second in charge—and had been impressed. Mary was bustling around with starched efficiency, slightly miffed that she'd missed the day's excitement. She was delighted with the opportunity to be used as an acute nurse and Amy would have no problem leaving all her patients in her charge.

'I have some office work to do…'

'No, you don't,' Kitty said blithely, as Joss fastened a dressing over her thumb. 'Amy works too hard, Dr Braden. Make her go home.'

'Tell you what,' he suggested. 'I'll stop at the store and cook for both of us.'

'You?'

'Me.' Once again she'd caught him unprepared and he reacted with ego. 'I can cook, and I need to do something to pay for my lodging.'

'I think you've done enough. One Caesarean. A healthy mum, a gorgeous baby and four treated residents…'

And one secretary minus her splinter—who was matchmaking for all she was worth. 'I'll donate a bottle of wine,' Kitty said blithely, beaming from Amy to Joss and back again. 'Mum gave it to me because she doesn't like it—and I can't think of an occasion more splendid.'

'Kitty—'

'More splendid than a welcome to Iluka's new doctor.'

'Hey, I'm only here until it stops raining,' Joss said uneasily, and Kitty beamed.

'Then long may it keep raining.'

'Keep your wine to stop you thinking about your thumb,' Amy suggested, and Kitty shook her head.

'Nope. I've been thinking about my thumb for four days now and suddenly it's better.'

'The anaesthetic hasn't worn off,' Joss warned, but Kitty would have none of it.

'Go on. Shoo, the pair of you. Have a wonderful night.' And as she pushed Amy out the office door and closed it after them she was crossing every finger and every toe. 'For a change,' she said.

Amy didn't go home at once. 'I'm not travelling in a pink Volkswagen even if you are,' she told Joss. 'And besides, I want my car at home. I'm not leaving it here.'

She wanted her independence. She certainly didn't want to be stuck out at White-Breakers with no way of getting back here but to be driven by Joss. So she sent him homewards and did a bit of busy work around the place—and finally popped in to see Charlotte.

The young mother was just waking. Marie was still on watch, and Mary was hovering nearby. Amy signalled them to disappear for a while. Charlotte should be up to talking but the last thing she wanted was a crowd.

'Feeling better?'

Charlotte gave her a wan smile. Her baby was sleeping beside her in a makeshift cot made out of a filing cabinet drawer and a television stand. It served the purpose, however. The little one looked blissfully content.

'I am...a bit.'

Amy pulled up a chair and smiled sympathetically at the new mother. 'You can say you feel lousy if you feel lousy.'

'OK, then. I feel lousy.'

'Dr Braden's written you up for pain relief. You can have something now.'

'I'll wait a while. I'm having enough trouble as it is, getting my head around...what's happened.'

'Is there someone you'd like us to contact?' Amy asked her gently. 'Someone must be worried about you?'

'No.'

That was blunt. 'You're really on your own, then?'

'Yes.'

Amy hesitated but then pressed further. There was a pallor about the girl's face that spoke of deep-seated misery—not just the shock of the day's events. 'Charlotte, can I ask why you were in Iluka?'

'I came here...looking for someone.'

'And did you find him?'

'Her.' She closed her eyes. 'And yes. Yes, I did.'

'So you do know someone in Iluka.'

'No one who wants to know me.'

'Charlotte, can I help you?' Impulsively Amy reached out and took the girl's hand. No one should be alone like this—especially when she was hurting so badly. And the pain wasn't just from the head wound and the effects of the Caesarean. The pain was soul deep. 'Let me close,' she urged. 'Tell me what's going on.'

'No.' The girl's face was shuttered and closed and she pulled away her hand.

Amy backed off. The last thing she wanted was to put more pressure on her. 'OK. I'm here if you want me.'

'How long am I stuck?'

'The river's in full flood. It may be up to a week before there's access, but you need a week in bed anyway. For now you must lie back and let your body recover—for your daughter's sake if not for your own.'

The girl looked down at her sleeping baby and her face twisted in something that was close to despair. 'She is beautiful, isn't she?'

'Yes, she is.' Amy looked down at the perfect little girl and she could only agree. 'Have you thought of what you might call her?'

'I... I need to speak...'

'To her daddy?'

The girl's face closed and she bit her lip. 'No. I don't need to speak to him. I can make up my own mind.' She chewed her lip for a little and then looked again at her daughter. 'What do you think of Ilona?'

'Ilona?'

'It's Hungarian for beautiful.'

'Then it's perfect.' Amy put a finger down and traced the soft curve of the baby's cheek. 'Ilona. It's just right.'

'It's sort of... I mean, she was born in Iluka. Iluka—Ilona.'

'Then it's even more perfect.'

The girl's face flushed with pleasure and she smiled. For the first time Amy saw her as she could be—a truly beautiful woman. 'You really think so?'

'I really think so.' She rose. 'You need to sleep now but, before you do, can I bring you the telephone? Isn't there someone you want to contact?'

'I don't—'

'I'll bring you the phone anyway,' Amy told her, stepping in before she refused entirely. 'Then when there's no one else around, you can make up your own mind who you want to tell about Ilona.'

Amy came out of the room and found Joss waiting. He was leaning against the wall of the corridor with his arms crossed, looking like a man prepared to wait for however long it took. He looked like a man waiting for his wife to try

on a dress, she thought suddenly. He had just that proprietorial air.

The thought was stupid. Nonsense. She brought herself up
with an inward jolt. 'I thought I sent you home.'

'I don't always go when I'm sent.' He grinned down at
her and another image sprang to mind—a half-grown
Labrador who'd just brought her the next-door neighbour's
newspapers. He was pleased and guilty all at the same time.

He made her want to smile.

'You realise we don't have anything to eat now,' she said,
trying to sound cross. 'The general store closes at six and
there's nowhere else.'

'Hey, I've been and come back,' he told her, wounded. 'I
have a car full of supplies. I'm not silly. And I am hungry.'
Then his smile faded and he looked toward the closed door
of Charlotte's room. 'Any joy?'

'She's not saying anything.'

'Her name's Charlotte Brooke. The police sergeant got that
from her plates. He just rang in with the information. She
lives on the other side of Bowra.'

'She's a long way from home, then.'

'Sergeant Packer wants to know whether he should check
out the address—just in case someone's frantic about her.'

'She doesn't want anyone told.'

'And if someone reports her missing?'

'We'll worry about it then.' Amy frowned. 'But what do
you think? Do we respect her need for privacy?'

'It seems to me,' Joss said slowly, 'that if she wants privacy and a few days' thinking time—time out to come to
terms with everything that's happened to her—then maybe
we should respect that. It might be just what she needs. She's
not suicidal?'

'No.' Amy thought back to the girl's face as she'd looked
down at her little daughter. 'She's falling deeper in love with

her daughter every minute. I don't think she's making any plans to abandon her. She's named her Ilona.'

'Ilona…' Joss ran it over his tongue and smiled. 'I like it.'

'So do I.' Amy smiled up at Joss and suddenly thought, *Wow!* This felt good. It felt right—that she should smile up at him. There was some connection… Something she didn't really understand.

And she liked it that he'd come back. He was as concerned as she was about Charlotte, she thought, and that felt good, too.

But what on earth was she thinking of? She had no links to this man. As soon as the weather eased he'd be off.

She didn't want friendship.

Or rather—she did but she knew only too well that it'd hurt when it finished. As it had hurt leaving every friend she'd ever made outside the tiny population of Iluka.

'Are you ready to go home?' he asked. He was still smiling. She had to give herself an inward shake to escape the vague feeling of unreality. The feeling that here was sweetness she could sink into…

'Um… I'm still not travelling in your pink Volkswagen.'

'Daisy will be hurt.'

'Daisy will never know.'

'That you chose your wreckage-mobile over her fine automobile?'

'There are some choices that are easy,' she retorted, and turned her back on him to head for the car park. But part of her was thinking, Some choices are way too hard.

Joss followed her out to White-Breakers and she was aware of him following her every bit of the way.

Why on earth had she asked him to stay? she wondered. She could have insisted he stay with his father and stepmother. It would have been far less complicated.

But then he might not have felt obligated to donate his professional services...

He would have stepped in anyway, she thought. Joss wasn't a man to stand back and watch while the likes of Kitty suffered with a splinter under her thumb.

He was a thoroughly nice man.

No. He was a darned sight more than that.

He was gorgeous!

Oh, for heaven's sake. She was engaged, she thought savagely. Malcolm was in the wings. OK, Malcolm lived at Bowra and she didn't see him all that often but that didn't leave her any less engaged. Any less committed.

She was committed to Malcolm. She was committed to Iluka. Sometimes she was so darned committed that she wanted to scream.

Amy drove into her nine-car garage and Joss drove in beside her. The two crazy little cars looked incongruous in such a setting. This garage had been built to house stretch limos or Mercedes at the very least. Not one Just-On-Wheels and a pink Volkswagen.

At least it was better than empty, she thought. She found she was looking forward to tonight. Sharing the kitchen—such as it was—with Joss and his lovely dog.

Maybe she should get a dog.

Yeah. And buy dog food with what?

Six more years...

'Damn you,' she told her departed stepfather for what must be the thousandth time. 'But I'm sticking with this. You won't win completely.'

Then Joss was climbing out of his Volkswagen, his arms laden with carrier bags, and she forgot all about her stepfather. Because who could think of a mean old man while Joss was here?

'Do you want help to carry them?' she asked. Food. Real food! No soup and toast tonight. How wonderful!

Joss looked at her face and he grinned. Taking a woman out to a five-star restaurant had never felt so good.

'I'll carry them,' he told her. 'Otherwise I have a feeling they might be demolished by the time they reach the kitchen.'

She'd offered to help carry the bags. Joss had refused her offer and it was just as well. She'd have dropped the lot when she saw what was in front of her. She led the way, pushed open the kitchen door and stopped dead.

What…?

Daisy was some organiser, Joss thought with wry appreciation as he looked around the transformed kitchen. Wow!

Before it had seemed empty. Now it was almost too full.

Amy had given Joss a key and Joss had left it with Daisy when he'd returned to the hospital. In the time he'd been away it looked as if the whole town had paid a visit.

With furniture.

There was a dining table and twelve chairs. An overstuffed settee. About five squashy armchairs. A huge rich Persian carpet. A colour television, a stereo, a couple of standard lamps. A wide oak desk.

The room was enormous and now it looked as it should. The furniture was old-fashioned and mismatched but it was comfortable and good quality. Daisy had chosen with care and she'd obviously had a lot to choose from!

'What…?' Amy was practically speechless. She walked forward in disbelief.

'I wonder if they've done the bedrooms yet,' Joss mused. He walked out along the corridor, opened the doors and checked. 'Yep.' Two of the bedrooms—the one Amy had been using and the one she'd designated his—were now fully furnished. They both had new beds, complete with luxurious bedclothes. More armchairs. Dressing-tables, wardrobes, bedside tables…

There was even a big squashy dog-bed at the foot of his

bed. Bertram was already ensconced, looking up with doggy satisfaction as Joss entered. He rose and waggled his tail, but his sleepy demeanour said he'd been entertained very well—he'd had a very busy afternoon supervising all this activity.

'This is fantastic.' Joss smiled his appreciation as his dog loped over for a pat. '*They're* fantastic.'

'Um…' Amy had walked into the bedroom behind him. She looked as if she'd been struck by a piece of four by two and hadn't surfaced yet. 'Who's fantastic?'

'The combined residents of Iluka. When I told Dad and Daisy how you were living…'

'You told them?'

'Of course I told them.'

'You had no right,' she said, distressed. 'Joss, this is my business. How I live.'

'You spend your time looking after the town. It's about time the town looked after you.'

'But this furniture… I can't keep it.'

'Of course you can.'

'You don't understand.' She was close to tears, he thought. Her hands were pressed to her cheeks, as if fighting mounting colour. 'Trevor and Raymond and Lysle…'

'Who are Trevor and Raymond and Lysle?'

'My…my stepfather's nephews.'

'Ah.'

'I can't accept this,' she told him. 'I can't keep anything.'

'I don't understand.'

'The nephews… My stepfather left me nothing. Have you any idea what the land tax is on this place?'

'I can guess.' In truth, he knew. Thanks to his father. The phones in Iluka had been running hot all day.

'And the land tax on the land beneath the nursing home?' she was saying. 'The overheads?' Still she was pressing her face. 'The nephews took everything I didn't own personally, and anything I do own has to be sold to keep the bank happy.'

'So what does that have to do with this?'

'I can't accept. Even if I did I'd have to sell—'

'This isn't a gift,' he said gently. He took her shoulders and steered her back to the kitchen. Bertram was shifting his sleepy body to the rug before the range and she thought suddenly, It's warm. It's warm!

But Joss was still speaking. 'Everyone at Iluka has moved here from somewhere else,' he told her. 'It's a retirement village so most people have built houses that are smaller than they're used to. Daisy says there's hardly a retiree who doesn't have something that they can't bear to sell but that doesn't fit easily into their new home. So this furniture is on loan. For as long as you need it.'

'But I can't—'

'You can. Hell, Amy, you work your butt off for these people. Allow them to repay it a little.'

'But...' She stared wildly around and focussed on the stove. There was a kettle on the hob, gently hissing steam. 'How long have you had the stove on? And the heating? I can't afford to pay for all this.'

'The heating's my lodging fee,' he told her. 'It's self-interest on my part. I have a conference paper to write and I don't like being cold. So I rang up the gas board and gave them my credit-card details. There's at least a six-month supply of gas been credited to your account. You can't use my rent to pay unimportant things like land tax. Oh, and speaking of land tax...'

'Yes?' She was so dazed she could hardly speak.

'My father's been on to Jack Trotter, the Shire President. The councillors had an emergency meeting this afternoon— in your kitchen.'

'Here?'

'Yes.'

'I don't believe this.'

'You should have let them know. Amy, they were horrified to see how you were living. The whole district wants to help. They voted unanimously to waive land tax on White-Breakers and the nursing home for the next six years. Retrospectively. They can't backdate it any more than a year but last year's tax will be refunded.'

Amy was practically speechless, but she was becoming angry. 'Joss, this is none of your business. I should never have let you near the place.'

'Then that would have been a great shame. I'm sorry to have to tell you this but your time as a martyr is over.'

He was enjoying this, she thought. A genie granting three wishes couldn't have looked any more placid than Joss Braden.

'You can't...'

But he was smiling. 'I already have.' He pulled a cheque from his pocket and handed it over. 'Mrs Hobbs from the general store asked me to give this to you. I gather she's the Shire treasurer.'

She looked down at the figure on the cheque and gaped. 'This is crazy. And as for you paying the gas... You know I didn't intend charging you rent. You mustn't.'

'It's been done,' he said virtuously. 'You try getting refunds from the Gas Corporation. Good luck is all I can say.'

Heat. She had heat. She had furniture. And enough money for essentials.

She had Joss, and a dog.

'Now to dinner,' he told her, lifting her chin with one long, strong finger. 'Bertram's hungry, even if we're not. Are you hungry?'

She couldn't take it all in. All she could absorb was the question.

Was she hungry?

'I'm starving,' she told him and it was the truth. She was.

'Good. Let's eat.'

*   *   *

It was the strangest meal. Joss had brought one of Mrs Hobbs's famous beef pies, and he had side dishes to match. Amy ate as she hadn't eaten for months—no, years—and all the time Joss watched her with that curious look of complacency.

'You look like a Scout who's just received his knot certificate—and I'm your very tricky knot,' she complained, and he grinned.

'I can see that. A knot, huh? Would you like some lemon meringue pie? Mrs Hobbs threw it in free.'

'Does the entire population of Iluka see me as their do-a-good-deed-to-Amy project?' she asked cautiously, and his grin widened.

'Don't knock it. It'll be a damned sight more comfortable than the way you've been living for the last four years. Why no one did anything about it...'

'Yeah. You come sweeping into town—'

'Guns blazing.'

'Ego blazing,' she retorted, and he chuckled.

'Egos are good for something. Does Malcolm have an ego?'

'Malcolm?'

'Your fiancé.'

'I know who Malcolm is,' she snapped. 'And, no, as a matter of fact, he doesn't have an ego.'

'That's why he hasn't come to the rescue of his maiden in distress.'

'I'm not in distress.'

'You are. Or you were. You know, a knight in shining armour with ego to match can sometimes be a very good thing. He gets things done.'

'Because he rides roughshod over people.'

'I haven't ridden roughshod over anyone,' he said gently, and her indignation took a step back. OK, he hadn't. Or...he had but in such a way...

'Um…'

'Wrap yourself around your lemon meringue pie,' he told her kindly. 'We don't want to upset Mrs Hobbs, now—do we?'

'No.' Of course she didn't.

But it wasn't Mrs Hobbs she was thinking of.

CHAPTER FIVE

AFTERWARDS Joss helped Amy with the dishes and then settled himself down at the table with his briefcase and laptop.

'Sergeant Packer rescued these, but the rest of my luggage is matchsticks,' he told her sadly. 'All I'm wearing is courtesy of my dad.' He looked ruefully down at the splendid example of Daisy's handiwork on his chest. 'Fair Isle sweaters aren't really my thing.'

'I think you look very...fetching,' she managed, and he glowered.

'Fetching what?'

'Fetching not very high stakes in fashion contests?' she ventured, and ducked as a wad of paper sailed across the room and hit her on the forehead. 'Ow.'

'You asked for that.'

'Hey, I like your sweater,' she said, laughing, and his glower deepened. But he didn't want to glower. She was smiling across the room at him and he wanted...

Damn, he knew exactly what he wanted, but the lady was engaged to be married. He was a guest in her house.

He couldn't.

'At least Sergeant Packer retrieved my briefcase,' he managed, and he wondered if she'd heard that his voice sounded odd. For heaven's sake, what was the matter with him? He was behaving like a schoolboy.

'You really do have a conference to prepare for?'

'Hey, that's what I told Dad and Daisy. Do you think I'd lie?'

'Only if you couldn't get what you want any other way.'

He tried a glare but it didn't come off. She was gorgeous! But he had to stay serious. He had to concentrate on something other than that beautiful smile. 'She's maligning me, Bertram.' Joss bent and fondled his dog's velvety ears. 'You hear that? I cook her a meal to die for and she maligns me.'

'There you go again. Who cooked the pies?'

'Mrs Hobbs might have,' he admitted grudgingly. 'But who fetched them. At great personal cost.'

'Personal cost?'

'I had to drive a pink Volkswagen.'

'There is that.' Then she frowned as the front doorbell pealed. 'Who on earth...'

'Maybe it's another sofa,' Joss told her. 'Daisy told me there was more to come.'

'Another sofa? How many do you think I need?'

It wasn't another sofa. It was a crate of good china, with a problem attached.

'I thought I'd drop these in and ask...'

Amy knew Marigold Waveny well. Her husband, Lionel, was the kite builder in the nursing home, and since Lionel and his kites had removed themselves from her ultra-neat home she'd never been happier. Neither had Lionel. Sometimes Amy wondered whether he'd feigned his senility to get more room for his kite-making. He and Marigold were still happily married—possibly much happier apart than they'd ever been together. Marigold spent her days at the nursing home, admiring kites, but at night she returned to her immaculate little home where there wasn't a kite in sight.

'I would have brought these earlier,' she told them, handing over her box to Joss with gratitude. 'But I was... I wasn't very well. I had my phone switched to the answering machine so I didn't hear about what Daisy was organising until just now.' She gave Joss a shy smile. 'Then I thought, Of course, I have all this china that I don't even like.'

Amy lifted a cup and gasped. 'Marigold! It's Royal Doulton. It's beautiful.'

'You enjoy it. Heaven knows, you do enough for my Lionel.'

'I wouldn't be brave enough to use it,' Amy told her, and Marigold shook her head.

'I have Royal Doulton, too,' she told them. 'But not such a loud pattern. This belonged to Lionel's mother, and if you dropped it I'd be very pleased. And I thought…' The voluble little lady faded to silence for a minute and then worked up courage. 'I thought…if I brought something…a gift…while the doctor was here…'

'Yes?' Joss was ushering her into the kitchen while she was speaking. His eyes were twinkling and he was smiling at Amy over the top of the elderly lady's head. He'd been a doctor for long enough to know what was coming. 'You didn't need to bring a gift to speak to me.'

'No, but I thought…'

'Tell us, Marigold,' Amy prodded, and Marigold took a deep breath and started.

'Well…'

'Well?'

'I think… I think I'm dying.'

Joss blinked. He set down the carton of china and thought about it. 'You what?'

'I just…' She shook her head as if trying to get rid of something. Get rid of terror? 'My heart's failing,' she whispered. 'It's going to stop. I can feel it. I'm dying and who cares about fancy china then?'

She stared wildly from Joss to Amy and back again—and burst into tears.

Finally they got it out of her—the reason for her terror. She was sitting in one of Amy's new chairs while Amy knelt before her, holding her hands, and Joss listened. And watched.

'I've been so tired,' she told them. 'For weeks I've been so tired I feel like I'm about to fall over. But when I go to bed at night I can't sleep. I just lie there and my heart hammers and hammers and I get so upset… I have thumping in my chest—it's thumping now. The palpitations are awful. I can't seem to get enough breath. Everything's just too much effort. I try... I've been going into the nursing home every day to see Lionel but it's been too much. Today I felt so dreadful I didn't go.' She looked distressfully at Amy. '*I didn't go!*'

She should have realised, Amy thought ruefully. Marigold spent every day at the nursing home and today Amy hadn't even missed her. It was just...well, today had been different.

Lionel hadn't realised—but, then, Lionel had been taken up by a new kite and Joss's dog.

'I stayed in bed,' Marigold told them. 'But it didn't help. My heart's thumping just the same. And it hurts. I thought... I thought I might die carrying that box but then I thought at least I'd die on the doctor's doorstep and not at home by myself.'

Gee, thanks, Amy thought wryly. Just what every home needs—a corpse on the doorstep.

But Joss kneeled beside her, and his expression said he was taking this deadly seriously. He took Marigold's wrist loosely between thumb and middle finger, counting her pulse as he glanced at his watch. His brow was furrowed in concentration.

'Do we have a stethoscope, Amy?' he asked, and she nodded and rose. Her bag was by the door—she acted as district nurse so she always had her bag handy.

'Am I going crazy?' Marigold whispered.

'I don't think you're going crazy.' Joss was watching her closely, his mind obviously in overdrive. 'You're very thin. Have you always been this thin or have you lost weight recently?'

'I've lost a bit,' she admitted, looking fearfully up at him. 'I'm so tired. I can't be bothered cooking.'

'So you've lost weight and you're constantly tired?'

'I *am* seventy-three, dear.'

'You're a spring chicken compared to those in the nursing

home.' He tilted her chin and ran his hand down her throat, gently feeling. 'Mrs Waveny, do you have any family history of thyroid trouble?'

'I…' She thought about that and finally nodded, not sure what he was getting at. 'Maybe I do. My mother had to take iodine for something. Would that be it?'

'Maybe it would.' Amy handed Joss a stethoscope, and he held it to Marigold's chest and listened. There was silence. Bertram wuffled and snuffed beside the fire, a dog at peace, but there was no peace on Marigold's face.

'It's bad, isn't it?' she whispered as Joss finished listening.

Joss hesitated, thinking it through. He wasn't a physician. He was a surgeon, for heaven's sake—but he was practically sure he was right.

'Marigold, you have what we call atrial fibrillation,' he told her. 'It's a fast, irregular heartbeat.'

She gasped. 'Is that bad?'

'It's not good. But I don't think you're dying. I suspect…' Once more he ran his hands down her throat, feeling the swelling. 'I suspect you have an overactive thyroid. I can't be sure until we run a blood test—which I'd imagine we can't do here—but for the moment I'm going to assume that's the case.'

'I… The thyroid is causing heart failure?'

'You don't have heart failure. Your heart isn't failing— it's just running on overdrive. Now, I'm not certain, but you have all the signs. You're tired, your neck seems a little swollen. You're short of breath, you're agitated, you have pains in the chest and you have a fast, irregular heartbeat. If I'm right—if this is just an overactive thyroid—then it can be controlled with tablets.'

She stared, torn between disbelief and hope. 'You're kidding.'

'I'm not kidding.'

There was a silence while she took that on board, her face lighting up by the moment.

'I'm not mad?'

'You're not mad.'

'Then what do I do about it?' She gazed from Joss to Amy and then back again. 'I guess…forget about it until I can see the doctor from Bowra?'

'No.' Joss shook his head. 'Marigold, we can't completely rule out heart disease, and until we do then we assume the worst. If you had someone living with you, maybe you'd be OK, but as it is you need to stay at the nursing home until we have some answers.'

'But…' Her distress level was rising again. 'I *will* be able to go home again?'

'Of course.' He rose and took her hand, pulling her up after him. 'If you like, I'll drive you home now. We'll pick up a nightie and a toothbrush and I'll take you in to hospital. I'd imagine Amy has Lanoxin in the drug cupboard? Am I right, Amy?'

'Sure.' She was almost as dumbfounded as Marigold.

'Great. Lanoxin slows your heart rate, Marigold. It'll make you feel a whole heap better—and we'll give you some sleeping pills, too, so you can get a decent sleep tonight. The combination will make you feel fantastic. Is it OK with you if you leave your car here? There's a bed available, isn't there, Amy?'

'I…yes.' Amy felt as stunned as Marigold looked at the speed with which things were being organised.

'There's no need—' Marigold started, but Joss shook his head.

'There is a need,' he said firmly 'Amy, will you ring Mary and let her know we're coming? Let's go now.'

Just like that…

Amy was left staring out at the departing pink Volkswagen feeling hornswoggled.

She would have coped.

Maybe she would have coped. If Marigold had come to

her, she would have popped her into hospital and rung the doctor in Bowra. But Marigold wouldn't have come to her.

There was a huge difference in people's attitudes to a nurse and a doctor. The locals knew Amy was overworked and they knew she only had nurse's training. If Joss hadn't been here, Marigold would have waited. If it had been heart disease...

It could well have been a disaster.

Iluka needed a doctor.

It was never going to have one, Amy thought sadly. Joss would leave and they'd be back to where they'd started. But for now...

But for now, she'd eaten better than she had for months, she had a warm, comfortably furnished house, a doctor caring for her patients.

She felt so good she could almost burst.

'Let's go for a walk,' she told Bertram, picking up pad and pencil and scribbling Joss a note. She needed to walk some of this happiness off before Joss returned.

It was still raining.

'That's what raincoats, galoshes and umbrellas are for,' she told Bertram. She looked at the dog's eager face and knew without being told that Bertram was as eager for a walk as she was.

'Then what are we waiting for?' She took a deep breath. 'I need to get rid of some energy. Get rid of... I don't know. Something. Because otherwise your master's going to walk in the front door and I'll kiss the guy.'

And that would never do. Would it?

Joss returned to find Amy gone.

'Bertram and I are at the beach,' the note told him. He stared at it for a while as if he didn't know what to do with it.

He had work to do.

He'd just done some work. Marigold was nicely settled in a room next to Lionel. She felt wonderfully at home, she had a diagnosis that she could cope with, her husband was by her side and she was with friends.

Would that city hospitals could be this good.

Could he ever be happy as a country doctor? He thought about it. Tonight had felt good. The whole damned thing. Hospitals where everyone knew each other...

But this would be an impossible place to set up a practice.

Whoa! What was he thinking about? Setting up here as a country doctor? He was a surgeon. He lived in the city.

Amy was here.

Amy was engaged to be married.

The whole damned thing was a figment of a stupid fancy. Get a grip, Braden, he told himself. What the hell was happening to him?

Amy was happening to him. Quite simply she was the most gorgeous woman he'd ever met. She affected him as no one else had ever done.

He didn't react to women this way.

Women were ancillary to his life. He'd decided that long ago. He liked having women around but he didn't do the love thing. The commitment. He had his father's example of what happened with commitment and there was no way he was travelling down that path.

So, tempting as it might be to commit himself to some woman—a house, babies, a mortgage, country practice...

No. It wasn't tempting in the least. So why was he thinking about it?

Maybe it was because Amy was so patently unavailable.

That was it, he decided, and he was a bit relieved to discover a reason. She was engaged to another man. She couldn't leave this place if she wanted to, so she was absolutely unattainable. Which was probably the reason he wanted her.

But that nice sensible reason didn't help much at all. He flicked on his laptop and stared down at his conference notes.

Life-threatening haemorrhage can be caused by aortic

dissection extending into the media of the aorta following a tear in the intuma, resulting in true and false lumina separated by an intimal flap...

What the hell was he talking about?

He'd written this a week ago. A lifetime ago. Tonight it wasn't making any sense at all, because tonight all he could think of was Amy.

She was down on the beach. With his dog. While he was sitting up here like a fool with some stupid conference notes that no one wanted to hear.

'They're important,' he told himself. They represented work he'd been committed to for the last three years.

'I'll worry about them when I get back to Sydney.'

'You told Dad and Daisy you needed to stay here to get them written.'

'So I lied. I stayed here to be near Amy.'

'Amy's engaged to another man.'

Damn.

He was going nuts, he decided. With a groan he pushed away his laptop, grabbed a coat that he'd seen hanging in the back porch and headed out the front door toward the beach.

The beach was wonderful. She always loved it. The seashore here was wild and windswept. In the summer millionaires parked their sunbeds here and concentrated on their tans but in winter she had it all to herself. The sand stretched away for miles in either direction. Her beach.

And tonight she had Bertram. That was special. The rain had eased a little—it was still stinging her face but not so much that she minded. She'd jogged down to the beach, Joss's dog loping beside her, and by the time she reached the sand she was warm and flushed and triumphant.

It had been a truly excellent day.

She'd helped deliver a baby. The weight of her financial need had been lifted by magic. She had furniture, she had heating, she had enough to eat...

'He's solved all my problems in one fell swoop,' she told Bertram, hurling a stick along the sand and watching in delight as the big dog went flying through the rain to fetch it back for what must surely be the hundredth time.

He loved it as much as she did.

Maybe she could get a dog.

Did Malcolm like dogs? She thought about that and decided probably not. Bertram hurled himself into the waves after another stick and came lunging back up the beach to her, then shook himself, sending seawater all over her.

No. Malcolm would definitely not like dogs.

Malcolm…

He hadn't rung tonight, she thought, frowning. He always rang, at seven every night. If he didn't find her at home he rang her at the nursing home.

Maybe the flooding had caused problems. Maybe the Bowra line was out of order.

She'd ring him when she got in. Or then again, maybe she wouldn't, she decided. It was ridiculous to speak to him on the phone every night. It was just a habit they'd got into.

Malcolm was just a habit.

No. Malcolm was just…Malcolm.

As opposed to Joss?

Now, that was a stupid way of thinking. When the rain ceased and a ferry could be established, Joss would be gone. Malcolm was all she had, so she should take care of the relationship.

She'd phone tonight.

Or tomorrow night.

Whatever.

She was a dark shadow outlined against the sea. The moon was struggling to emerge from behind clouds. There were faint glimmers breaking through, sending shards of silver light across the waves. Amy was tossing sticks for Bertram and Bertram was running himself ragged, wild with excitement.

Joss stayed where he was among the dunes, watching woman and dog. They made a great pair, he thought. Amy was enjoying herself. Her body language as she bent over the dog, as she stooped to lift his stick and throw...she was soaking in every minute of this.

She should have a dog of her own.

Where could he get her one?

That was a crazy thought. For heaven's sake, he didn't *know* that she liked dogs. Maybe she was just being polite.

He didn't think so.

She was...lovely.

But he was being stupid. Fanciful. This was a Cinderella type of situation, he told himself harshly. He was attracted to Amy because she was deserving and she was beautiful and she was unattainable. Would he be as attracted if she was available? Surely not.

She was committed to living in this dump for the next six years. What man would go near her knowing that?

Malcolm would. Obviously. And it wasn't such a dump.

'It's the ends of the earth.'

'This beach is lovely.'

'Look around,' he told himself harshly. The rain had stopped momentarily and the moon was full out. The beach stretched away for miles, as far as the eye could see. The moonlight played over the sodden sand, the wind whipped the waves into a frenzy and...

And nothing and nothing and nothing. There was only Amy and his dog. There was nothing else for miles.

Why would anyone ever come to this place through choice?

The millionaires did, he thought, looking back up the beach to the show of ostentatious wealth lining the foreshore. But the houses obviously belonged to those who valued their privacy. The millionaires came through choice. The elderly retirees who lived behind the sand dunes had come because they'd been conned.

This isolation must have been why Amy's stepfather had built the place, Joss decided. It would be why all these mansions had been built. There were no shops to speak of and even the retirees who lived here weren't provided for. Here there was absolute seclusion.

There'd be no children here spoiling the sand on sunny days—imposing their noisy presence on this super-wealth. In Australia, where it wasn't possible to own a private beach, this was the best this tiny pocket of elite millionaires could do. They'd built their houses and they were screwing the rest of the population to maintain their fabulous lifestyle. For six weeks a year.

He was getting bitter.

He was also getting cold, he thought, and gave himself a mental shake. He had better things to do than stand here and think about Amy's problems. He had a conference paper to write.

Ha!

The conference paper could wait. He took a deep breath and turned his face into the wind. Digging his hands deep into his pockets, he went to join his dog.

And Amy.

She saw him coming.

Joss was hunched into an ancient overcoat, and for a moment as he came down the sand hill toward him she had a vision of her father. The man who'd loved her and died, leaving her to her dreadful stepfather.

She'd loved her father. He'd been one special man.

'What?' He reached her and found she was smiling, but it was an odd sort of smile, tinged with sadness. 'You look like you've seen a ghost.'

'Maybe I have.' She pulled herself together. 'It's that coat.' She thought about not saying anything but then decided to tell him anyway. 'It was my father's—not my stepfather's but my father's. My mother kept it and then loaned it to Robbie. Robbie was our gardener.'

'You were fond of Robbie?'

'He's a lovely old man. My friend. I had to let him go— there's no money to keep him. One of the local farmers puts a couple of sheep on my grass now and that's the extent of my gardening. Meanwhile, Robbie's living in a council flat in Bowra and I know he's miserable. I tried to make him keep the coat but he wouldn't.' She gave a twisted little smile. 'He said to keep it until I can have him back again. As if... But I know he misses me as much as I miss him. And he's so broke. My stepfather should have set up a superannuation fund for him, but loyalty to his staff wasn't his style.'

'You don't sound like you spend much time polishing your stepfather's headstone.'

'I leave that for the nephews.'

'They loved him?'

'They loved his money.' She grimaced. 'Anyway, it's too good a night to think about my stepfather. Isn't this fabulous?'

Fabulous?

It had started to rain again and there was a cold trickle running down his nose. The wind was making a mockery of his hood—it had blown back and his hair was damp and windblown. The smell of the sea was all around them and the breakers were roaring into the night.

It was fabulous, he decided, and he glanced down at Amy and found her smile had changed.

'You like it, too,' she said on a note of satisfaction. 'I thought you would.'

'It's great.'

'There was no need for my stepfather and his cronies to make this beach so exclusive,' she said reflectively. 'You could have thousands of people here and still find a spot

where you can be alone. There's miles and miles of beach…'
She put back her arm and tossed Bertram's stick with all her
might along the beach. The dog put back his ears and flew.
'And it's all ours. Sometimes…sometimes I feel rich.'

'Hmm.'

'How can you bear to go back to Sydney?'

'I can't,' he said promptly. 'I think I'll stay here.'

'And become a beachcomber?'

'There are worse fates.'

'You wouldn't miss your surgery?'

Of course he would. They both knew it. Beachcombing
was a dream. Beachcombing with Amy.

'Do you want to walk out on the rocks?' she asked, seeing
Joss's face and having enough sense to change the subject.
'It's great—though you might get your feet wet.'

'Wetter,' he muttered. His shoes had sunk into the wet
sand and he could feel the damp creeping into his socks.
'Well, why not?'

'Excellent.' Amy grinned and grabbed his hand. 'Follow
me.'

The feel of her hand changed things.

Follow her…

She was leading him to a rocky outcrop which spiked up
out of the breakers. 'It's a bit dangerous,' she warned. 'If
you don't know where you're going, you can get into trouble.
So hang on.'

How could he do anything else?

A bit dangerous…

She needed her head read, he thought as she clambered
over the first of the rocks, towing him behind. There were
breakers smashing over the rocks in force. Back on the beach
Bertram stood and looked on in concern. There was no way
he was following and the look on his face said they were
crazy to try.

But she'd done this a thousand times before.

The first few rocks were the worst—the foam from the breakers was surging over the slippery surface and they had to time their way between waves. Even then they didn't quite make it—Joss ended up on the other side with shoes full of water.

'Don't tell me. It's low tide now and the next wave will carry us off to our doom. Or we'll be trapped with the tide rising inch by inch.'

'You've been reading too many adventure novels,' she said severely. '"The moon was a ghostly galleon, tossed upon stormy seas…" With moonrakers, pirates, chests and chests of jewels, and a heroine chained to the rocks as the tide creeps higher…higher..'

'I seem to remember,' he said faintly, 'that "The moon was a ghostly galleon" started a tale of a highwayman.'

'Same difference,' she said cheerfully. 'Same criminal hero and a dopey heroine abandoning all for love. But don't worry. The tide's full now so it doesn't get any worse than this, and I'm not about to end it all for anything. Look. Clear rock.'

It was, too. The outcrop of rock stretched right out into the bay, a breakwater in its own right. And where she was leading him now… It was a channel of rock. The rocks on both sides formed a barrier.

'It's like Moses and the Red Sea,' he said, stunned, and she grinned.

'Yep. The parting of the water. This is my very favourite place in the whole world and I love it best when it's just like this. Wild and stormy and wonderful.'

Joss didn't answer. He couldn't. Maybe it was because he was concentrating on keeping his footing on the slippery rocks—or maybe it was that he was just plain bemused.

Finally they reached the end—a vast flat rock perched high above the breakers. Amy released his hand to scramble up the last few feet, leaving him to follow. When he found his feet she was standing right at the end, staring into the moonlight.

The shafts of moonlight were playing over her face. She looked up and he thought that he'd never seen anything so lovely.

'*He makes bright mischief with the moon…*'

Where had that come from?

Wherever—from a poem deep in the recesses of his schoolboy reading—it suddenly seemed apt.

Only the pronoun was wrong.

She makes bright mischief with the moon.

Amy would be happy wherever she was, whatever she did, he thought. She made the most of her life. She cared.

She was soaked to the skin. Her braid had come unfastened and her curls were a tangled riot around her face. She was wearing a coat that was too small and clothes that were too old—and she was turning her face into the wind as if she'd been given the world.

It was too much. It would have been too much for any man.

He took her hands in his as if to steady himself, and when her body twisted toward him he pulled her close.

He kissed her.

Of course he kissed her. There was a compulsion happening here that he had no hope of controlling. He couldn't even try.

She was so desirable. So beautiful. So…

He didn't know. But there was a damp tendril coiling down her forehead that he had to push softly away. There was salt water on her face that he had to taste… And her lips were soft and pliant and…and waiting.

Waiting for him.

She was so lovely.

His woman…

'Lady, by yonder blessed moon I swear…'

Moon madness. That's what this was—the same blessed moon that had caused Romeo to forsake all for his Juliet.

For heaven's sake, he was a surgeon—not a poet!

But he was a poet tonight. Who wouldn't be with such sweetness in his arms.

Amy was so right for him. It was as if a part of him had been missing and had found its way home. Each curve of their bodies fitted together as if they knew each other through and through.

Joss held her close and deepened the kiss—because nothing, ever, had felt so right before.

And Amy?

What was she doing? she thought wildly. She'd taken this man to her very special place—her place—the place where she'd sobbed her heart out as a child or come when life had been just too bleak for words. It was a place of sanctuary and of healing.

She hadn't expected this to happen.

To fall in love…

Because that was what was happening. As though responding to a force beyond her control, she opened her lips to the man who held her. More. She opened her heart.

It was so right! Her body was melting into his—aching—wanting and welcoming.

She felt herself sinking into him. Desperate to deepen the kiss. Desperate to grow closer. Though how could they be closer than they were at this minute? Two halves of one sweet whole. They'd been torn asunder by some mystery of fate and could now come together for always.

Always.

Joss's hands were pulling her body ever closer. His kiss deepened and deepened again—and so did the wonder.

She was like no woman he'd ever kissed, he thought, dazed with the sensation of what was happening to him. And why? She was sodden with sea spray. She wore no trace of make-up and her clothes were shabby and her hair was blown every which way. There were trickles of rainwater running down her nose, merging with the rain on his face where their lips met. She looked about as far from his ideal woman as he could possibly imagine any woman being.

So how could she be meeting this need—this desperate desire—that until now he'd never known he had?

He didn't know. All he knew was that she was…Amy.

And that was enough.

And finally—*finally*—they pulled away, as pull away they had to. The waves were sloshing over their shoes, they were sodden and back on the beach Bertram was starting to bark his anxiety for the world to hear.

'We're worrying Bertram,' Amy managed, and her voice was a husky whisper, full of uncertainty.

'Worrying Bertram!' Joss tried to smile down at the confusion on her face. 'I'm worrying me.'

That worked. 'Hey, I don't have any infectious diseases.'

He smiled—but only just. 'Amy…'

But she put a finger on his lips to stop him saying more. 'Don't.'

'Don't what?'

'Apologise. It was a magic night. It *is* a magic night, and I always think magic nights should be sealed with a kiss. Don't you?'

'I don't understand,' he said, dazed. 'Amy, what the hell happened there?'

'An electric charge?' Her smile was returning. 'Moonbeams and water. They pack a lethal charge.'

They certainly did. 'Amy, I never meant…'

'Of course you didn't,' she said cordially. 'And neither did I. But Bertram thinks we did and seeing as he's acting as our chaperon I think we should go back to him. Don't you?'

'Yes.' Of course he did. After all, he was cold and he was wet. Why on earth would he want to keep standing here?

He did. Badly.

But she was more in control than he was. 'Let's go,' she told him, her voice firming as she took his hand to lead him back to the beach. 'I have a fiancé to telephone and you have a conference to prepare for.'

Right. Right!

Bertram was waiting for them to return to the beach. His conference paper was waiting to be written. The unknown Malcolm was waiting in Bowra.

His life was waiting for him to get on with it.

But how the hell was a man to concentrate on writing a conference paper after that? Joss showered and changed into more of his father's clothes—he'd kill for another pair of jeans, he decided, and wondered for about the thousandth time how Amy put up with no shops. Dried and warm, he returned to the kitchen to find Amy had disappeared.

'I've gone to bed,' the note on the table read. 'Make yourself some cocoa.'

Right. Cocoa. When what he needed was…

Sex?

No. Not sex. Or not just sex.

He wanted Amy.

It was nine o'clock. After the day he'd had he should be exhausted. Maybe he should go to bed, but as he wandered down the passage he heard the shower running in Amy's bathroom. A vision appeared unbidden…

Whoa. Unless he was careful here, he'd have to take another shower. This time cold.

Bertram was nosing at Amy's bedroom door, whimpering to be let in to visit someone he'd decided very firmly was a friend, and Joss took his collar and pulled him away.

'No. We're not wanted, boy. She has a fiancé.'

It was just as well she did, he decided. The last thing he wanted was a tie that could hold him to Iluka. It was bad enough that he had a father here and he'd have to visit every few months.

But Amy was here.

The sound of the shower ceased. She'd be drying herself.

'Oh, for heaven's sake, Braden, get a grip. You're a grown man.'

'Yeah, with grown man urges.'

'She doesn't want you.'

'I could just towel her back…'

He was a guest in her house. He wasn't wanted. He had a bed of his own to go to.

The phone rang and he hesitated, half expecting—half hoping—Amy would open the door and come out to the kitchen to answer it. And then he realised it was ringing in her bedroom. Damn, she had an extension. What business did she have, having an extension when she was broke?

He was losing his mind.

But he didn't move. He sort of listened—just for a minute.

And from the other side of the door he heard, 'Malcolm. How lovely. I was worried about you.'

Damn.

He took himself firmly in hand and took himself off to his bed. Alone. She was worried about Malcolm?

He was worried about himself!

Amy had herself under control—sort of—and was answering the phone to her fiancé. What had gone on tonight with Joss was an aberration, she told herself firmly. It had nothing to do with her or with her future. It had only been a kiss.

Which was why she'd made a dash to her bedroom and had locked the door, thankful that her room had an *en suite* bathroom so she didn't have to face Joss again tonight.

It was only a kiss, she said to herself like a mantra. A kiss with no future.

Her future was here in Iluka. Her future was with Malcolm. Now he'd phoned, as she'd known he would— though it was really unusual for him to ring two hours late.

'I was worried,' she told him, striving to keep her voice

light. 'When you didn't ring I thought the telephone lines might be down.'

'No. The lines are fine. But I hear you've lost the bridge.' Malcolm sounded strained, she thought. Unlike him.

'Yes. We're stranded but we're fine. Though there was one casualty…'

'A casualty?' Still that note of anxiety.

'No one we know. A young woman crashed her truck and she was in full labour. She ended up having her baby here in the nursing home.'

'A baby?' His voice rose in disbelief and Amy thought, He really is worried. For some reason he sounded terrified.

'She's fine, Malcolm. We all are. David Braden's son is here and he's a doctor. He was trapped when the bridge came down and Joss is a fine surgeon. He did a Caesarean, delivering a beautiful little girl, and now he's on the spot for any medical needs we might have.'

There was a silence while Malcolm thought that through, then he said, 'So…the woman's fine. And the baby?'

'Great. Malcolm, is there anything wrong?'

'No. No. Did the woman say…who she was?'

Amy frowned. Charlotte hadn't exactly given permission for her name to be broadcast. If it hadn't been for the policeman tracking of her licence plates, they still wouldn't know it. 'For some reason I don't think she wants her identity known.'

'Oh.'

'But I'm afraid she's as stuck here as we all are. I guess they'll organise a ferry over the river soon.'

'Yeah.'

'You sound…odd.'

'Do I?' There was another lengthy silence from the end of the line then he added, 'It must be the distance or something. Water in the line.'

'Is everything OK at your end?' she asked.

'Why wouldn't it be?'

'No reason.' But still she had this niggle of a doubt. He sounded distracted.

'You're OK yourself?' He still sounded strained.

'I'm fine,' she said gently. 'Just a bit tired. It's been a long day. Goodnight, Malcolm.'

For some reason he was as eager as she was to end the conversation. 'Goodnight,' he told her, and hung up—leaving her staring at the receiver.

What on earth was going on?

Amy went to bed but she didn't sleep. She lay awake and stared at the ceiling, thinking of a kiss.

This didn't make any sense. The kiss and how she was responding to it didn't make sense at all.

When Malcolm kissed her it didn't feel like this.

Maybe it was because Joss was forbidden fruit, she thought bleakly. You always wanted what you couldn't have—and she couldn't have Joss.

Maybe she could open her bedroom door...

Oh, yeah, great. What was she thinking of? A spot of seduction?

'I wouldn't mind,' she told herself honestly and then bit her lip. Where would that lead her? To a broken engagement and desperate unhappiness when Joss left.

As he surely would.

'But I could just have fun—for a while. For a few short days while the bridge is down...'

Fun? She'd never had fun. She'd forgotten the meaning of the word. From the time her father had died the world had become a dangerous and threatening place, where the only way to survive was sheer, grinding hard work.

She had six years to go.

And after that? Marriage to Malcolm...

They might even marry earlier, she thought, and there was a note of desperation entering her thoughts now. Malcolm had been pushing for them to marry straight away. He'd have to stay in Bowra as his practice was there, and she was stuck at Iluka, but he could come at weekends. A weekend marriage...

It didn't excite her at all.

Malcolm didn't excite her.

'It's because he's familiar,' she told the dark. She knew him as well as she knew a pair of old socks. But... She thought about it. Tonight he'd been different. Not different in the way Joss was different but different all the same.

She didn't know what had got into Malcolm tonight.

'Maybe I don't know all there is to know about him. Maybe he'll turn into a James Bond in disguise. Or a Joss...'

The thought made her smile.

But it didn't make her go to sleep—and it wasn't Malcolm she was thinking about as she tossed and turned in the night.

It was very definitely Joss.

Joss had had a huge day. He'd almost been killed, he'd almost been swept away in the river, he'd fallen in love...

Hey! Where had that come from?

'You're imagining things,' he told the dark. Love? What did he know about love?

He only knew that Amy was the most beautiful woman he'd ever met.

But she wasn't beautiful, he decided, trying to see things dispassionately. Not in the conventional way. She was too careless of her appearance to be classed as beautiful.

But when she smiled...

'Beautiful,' Joss told his pillow, and he groaned as he turned over yet again and tried for elusive sleep. 'Just beautiful.'

At two in the morning the phone rang. Joss was still awake, so he heard it, and he heard Amy's soft voice answering. Something at the hospital? By the time Amy knocked at his door he was already reaching for his father's spare dressing-gown.

'Problems?'

It was hard to concentrate on problems. He didn't have his lamp on and Amy was lit by the hall light. She was wearing a long nightgown, trailing down to bare feet. It was cut low in the front and her curls were wisping down to her breasts. It was the first time he'd seen her with unbraided hair and the sight almost took his breath away. She looked sort of ethereal. Gorgeous...

But she was already hauling her hair back into a knot, ready for what lay ahead. 'Joss, can you help?'

That was what he was there for. He was almost grateful to be asked. Any more staring into the dark and he was in danger of losing his mind.

Any more staring at the woman in front of him and he'd definitely lose his mind.

'What's wrong?'

'A child. A little girl...'

He stared at that. 'A child? In Iluka?'

'We do have them. Just not many. Margy Crammond has her granddaughter staying with her. Emma's six years old and she's woken feeling dreadful. Margy says she can't walk.'

'Yeah?' He tossed aside his dressing-gown, hauled off his pyjama jacket and reached for his dad's Fair Isle sweater. His mind shifted straight into emergency mode. He was already sifting and discarding diagnoses, so much so that he didn't even wince as the amazing patterned sweater slipped over his head. Joss was a doctor first and foremost, and an emergency had him putting everything else aside.

Or almost. Amy's damned negligee was almost transparent...

Concentrate!

'What do you think the options are?' he asked. 'Hysteria?' Paraplegia in children was so unusual the first suspicion was a psychological diagnosis rather than a physical one.

But Amy was shaking her head. 'Margy seems to think

it's something more serious. Hysteria would be unusual at two in the morning—though she is homesick. She's been staying with her grandparents for a week and was supposed to be going home today. She's a bit upset that she can't. But Margy said she was sound asleep a couple of hours ago when they went to bed and she's woken in trouble.'

Hell! He thought about the possibilities—in a place where there were no acute facilities—and he didn't like them one bit. 'I'll go. Where is she?'

'*We'll* go,' Amy told him. 'This is my town. My people.'

'And you have work tomorrow.'

'*We'll* go,' she said again in a voice that told him he might as well save his breath. She wasn't listening to arguments. 'Half a minute while I pull on some jeans.'

CHAPTER SIX

THIS was not hysteria.

Emma Crammond was one sick little girl. By the time they reached Margy and Harry Crammond's house, the girl's grandmother was beside herself with worry and her grandfather was coming a very close second.

'She can't make anything work,' Margy told them as she led them through the house. She glanced up at Joss with gratitude. The whole town knew who Joss was now. News travelled fast in a small community. 'Oh, Dr Braden, thank heaven you're here. She looks just awful.'

She did.

The child was still in bed, but she was wide-eyed and frantic. Her breathing was fast and furious—as if she'd just run a marathon—but by her skin pallor Joss could see that she wasn't getting enough oxygen no matter how hard she breathed. Even from the doorway he could see that she was cyanosed, her skin taking on the tell-tale bluish tinge arising from inadequate oxygen.

What on earth was wrong?

They'd travelled in Amy's car. Joss usually travelled with a basic medical kit but it had been pulped along with the rest of the rear of his car. So he was dependent on Amy. 'Do we have oxygen?' he asked, expecting the worst, but Amy was nodding, moving already back to the front door.

'Yes. I'll get it.'

She had more than just oxygen. She had a complete and extensive medical kit.

She was back in seconds, handing Joss a stethoscope as she hauled out the oxygen mask to attach to the cylinder by her side. Whew, Joss thought—and then reminded himself that he should have expected no less. Amy obviously acted as district nurse and was first port of call in emergency for Iluka's elderly. Oxygen would be something she needed all the time.

So he had what he required. Now he could concentrate on the child. He needed to concentrate. Her illness was frightening.

'I can't...' The little girl was frantic. She was tossing wildly on the bed—as if trying to escape some unknown demon—and her grandfather was vainly trying to restrain her. 'My legs... I can't move them... Oh, I want my mummy.'

'Her mother's in Bowra.' Beside the bed, her grandmother was sobbing with fear. 'Dear God, what's wrong?'

'Emma, you must hush and keep still while the doctor works,' Amy told the little girl. She signalled to Harry to stand clear and sat on the bed. 'I'm fitting a mask over your face to help you breathe. But if you fight it, it won't help. You must keep still. Do you hear?'

The little girl nodded, but her terror was still almost palpable.

'We don't know what's wrong with you yet.' Amy was already sliding the mask over the little girl's face. 'But here we have Dr Braden who's stuck in Iluka like you are, because the bridge fell down. So we have our very own Iluka doctor. Isn't that lucky?'

Lucky? Yeah, great. Except he didn't know what was wrong with her. Hell, he was a surgeon, not a physician.

But he had gone through basic medical training. He'd worked for two years in an emergency department of a busy city hospital before he'd specialised—but this wasn't fitting into anything he'd ever seen.

The child was badly cyanosed. Her skin was growing more blue by the minute, which meant she still wasn't getting enough oxygen. Her heartbeat was rating 170 beats a minute and her breathing was far too fast. Yet she wasn't running a temperature. She was completely afebrile and both lungs sounded normal.

The oxygen didn't seem to be making a difference.

'What's she eaten tonight?' Joss asked. This wasn't making any sense.

'Just what we ate. Roast beef and veggies. Apple pie. Nothing else.'

'You're sure?'

'Yes.'

They'd have three patients here in a minute, Joss thought grimly, and sent an unspoken message to Amy with his eyes. They had to get the pressure off the elderly couple before they collapsed.

'We need to get Emma to hospital,' he told them. 'I want a chest X-ray. There must be something going on.'

But what?

'She's asthmatic,' Harry told Joss. He took that on board but still it wasn't making sense. 'It's only mild…' The old man gulped and swallowed a couple of times. 'I thought—I thought you should know.'

Asthma he could deal with, but this wasn't asthma. Still, it was something… 'OK. Amy, do we have salbutamol?'

'Sure.' Amy was already preparing it. She was a fine nurse, Joss thought. A wonderful team member. He could work alongside her any day.

'We'll give her salbutamol just to make sure,' Joss said, looking at the little girl's frantic eyes. He shook his head. 'But asthma…it doesn't make sense.'

Nothing did.

They drove Emma to the hospital in Amy's wreckage-mobile with Joss cradling the child in the back seat as he held the oxygen mask in place. They'd left her grandparents collecting her night things and contacting her mother—and pulling themselves together. The old people were shocked and shaky, and Amy rang their neighbours, asking them to drive the couple in. The neighbours just happened to be Joss's father and stepmother.

Amy didn't refer to Joss before she rang them. Joss had enough to worry about keeping Emma alive. David and Daisy were dependable and solid; she could rely on them to look after Emma's grandparents and she didn't want any more casualties tonight.

One was enough—and maybe even one was too many to save. By the time they reached the hospital things were deteriorating even further.

Amy found herself making silent pleas as she drove, and as she helped Joss lift Emma out of the car her pleas grew more desperate. Were they going to lose her?

Why? This was no asthma attack. What was going on?

Joss was agreeing with her. 'There's no way this is just asthma,' Joss muttered as they carried her swiftly through to X-Ray. The nursing home was settled for the night. It was darkened and at peace, and Sue-Ellen, the night nurse, emerged from the nurses' station, shocked at the startling interruption to her night.

Sue-Ellen, like Amy, had done her training in an acute hospital and she switched to acute care without a murmur. Joss couldn't have asked for a better team as they set up the drip, monitored the oxygen flow and organised the child for an X-ray.

Emma was still terrified. The most important thing had to be reassurance—but how to do that when they didn't know what they were dealing with?

The X-rays told them nothing. The X-rays were normal.

Hell, what? *What?*

Joss was raking his hair as he looked helplessly down at the child on the bed. 'We need blood tests. I don't suppose you have the facilities here…'

Amy shook her head, knowing what he needed was beyond them. 'We can do blood sugars and we have an oximeter to measure oxygen levels.'

'I want to do blood gases.'

'We can't.'

Hell!

He wanted his teaching hospital, he thought desperately. He wanted a specialist paediatrician and a pathologist. He wanted some answers...

The child was slipping into unconsciousness and he'd never felt so helpless.

'Joss?'

'Mmm.' He was holding the child's wrist, feeling her racing pulse. His mind was turning over and over. What...?

'Joss, the swab...' Amy sounded hesitant—unsure—and she caught Joss's attention.

What was she looking at? He followed her gaze.

He'd set up a drip before the X-ray, thinking that they might need adrenalin at any minute. The child couldn't keep this pulse rate up for ever, and the cyanosis was at dangerous levels. So he'd inserted a drip and placed tape over the back of Emma's hand to hold it steady. But the insertion site had bled a little. Amy had swabbed the blood away and the swab lay in a kidney dish. Sue-Ellen had lifted the dish out of the way but Amy was reaching to grip her hand.

Sue-Ellen paused, the dish with the swab held before her. The light was directly on it.

'It's brown,' Amy said stupidly, and she looked up at Joss. 'Surely that can't be right?'

He stared. There it was. The bloodstained swab had turned to a deep, chocolate brown colour.

No, it wasn't right, but there it was. Unmistakable.

Where had he read about that? Joss closed his eyes, his mind racing. Where...?

And there it was. An article studied for a long forgotten exam. Useless information suddenly resurrected.

'Methaemoglobinaemia.' Joss could hardly frame the word. He could barely remember it. But it must be. He stared at the swab as if he couldn't believe his eyes.

Amy was still confused. 'What?' She'd never heard the word. 'Methaem—'

'Methaemoglobinaemia. It's a type of acute anaemia caused by exposure to some sort of poison.' Joss could hardly take his eyes off the swab. 'I've never seen it before—I've only read about it. But some chemicals—some poisons—oxidise the iron in the blood, meaning the blood can't carry oxygen. That describes exactly what we've got here. Chocolate brown blood. I must be right. I can't think of anything else. Amy, get me Sydney Central. I want to talk to a haematologist. Tell them we want an expert in poisons—the best they have—and I don't care if you have to wake him up to speak to him. This is urgent.'

His mind was whirring over half-forgotten textbook cases. 'I'd guess activated charcoal or…' The article was becoming clearer in his mind as he spoke, forgotten texts somehow dredged up into memory. 'Do we have any methylene blue?'

'Methylene blue?'

'It's used to treat methaemoglobinaemia—when the blood can't deliver oxygen where it's needed in the body. It's also used as a dye to stain certain parts of the body during surgery.' What was the chance of having it in Iluka? Damn, why didn't they have a pharmacy? Though even a normal city pharmacy might not stock this.

Amy shook her head, dazed by the speed and certainty of his diagnosis. 'Methylene… I'll check. We're set up with emergency supplies so if the Bowra doctor's here she has everything she needs in the drug cupboard.'

'I think we might have something called that,' Sue-Ellen said diffidently. 'If I remember right. Dr Scott—the doctor from Bowra—gave us a list when we opened four years ago. She put all sorts of weird things on the list. I remember the pharmacist who supplied us scoffing and saying she was way out of date, and I think it was the methylene blue he was talking about when he said it.'

Please… 'Let's hope you're right,' Joss told her. 'But even

if you are, I don't know the dosage. Amy, get onto the phone. I need a haematologist with paediatric back-up. Now!'

What followed was an example of a medical community at its best.

Within five minutes Amy had a telephone link set up—a conference line with a paediatrician, a haematologist and a pathologist for good measure. They'd all been woken from sleep but their concern was audible through the teleconferencing link from Sydney.

They were fascinated as well as concerned. If we have to have a dangerous illness maybe it's as well to have an interesting one, Amy thought ruefully. All doors were open to a case of a perilously ill child with an unusual diagnosis.

The case conference was swift, intelligent and concise, and by the time Sue-Ellen had located a dated bottle of methylene blue from the back of the drug cupboard Joss was ready. While everyone held their breath—including the three specialists on the end of the phone—Joss administered fifty milligrams.

Then they waited. They all waited, and the specialists from Sydney stayed on the phone and waited with them. There was no appreciable change but at least Emma didn't get worse. She was drifting in and out of consciousness, fighting the oxygen mask every time she surfaced. More and more Amy wanted her mother to be there. In her mother's absence she cuddled the child herself.

After twenty minutes the combined opinion was to wait no longer. Thanking his lucky stars for a comprehensive drug cupboard—and that methylene blue didn't suffer a use-by date—Joss administered another twenty-five milligrams.

Then they stood back and waited again, and it was the hardest thing—dreadful—to do. To watch and wait as a child fought for life.

And then results.

At first they thought they were imagining it. There was a

combined holding of breath, and then they were almost certain. The awful blue was fading. The cyanosis was easing—just a bit, but enough to think that maybe...

Maybe was right. Another few minutes and they were sure. Emma was improving while they watched. The specialists on the end of the phone were jubilant, and so was everyone in the room. Sue-Ellen burst into tears, and it was all Joss and Amy could do not to join her.

Still they watched, but the child's agitation was settling. Her colour was improving by the minute. Her breathing was easing as the oxygen was finally reaching her blood. The danger was over.

'Look for a poison,' the haematologist growled, before disconnecting and returning to his bed. He was a gruff man but there was emotion in his gruffness. 'She must have eaten something that oxidises the ferrous iron in the blood. Sodium nitrate, maybe? Don't let the kid go home until you discover the source or you'll have her back in with another episode, and next time you mightn't be so lucky. And if anyone's eating where she's been eating, get them out of the house until you know where the hell it came from.'

He left them to it and went back to his bed.

There was the sound of a patient's bell from somewhere else in the nursing home. Life went on. Sue-Ellen made her escape, weeping audibly into her handkerchief, leaving Joss and Amy staring at each other in disbelief.

'Oh, thank God,' Amy murmured. Emma was drifting into an exhausted natural sleep, and her colour was almost back to normal. Amy had been cradling her to comfort her distress. Now the child's lashes had fluttered closed. Amy laid her back on her pillows and gently tucked her in.

'Do you want to tell her grandparents the good news?' Joss asked, and by his voice Amy could tell he was as shaken as she had been. Margy and Harry Crammond hadn't come into the room. They'd stayed out in Reception and panicked in isolation. Their distress had just upset their granddaughter more.

'You tell them.' Amy was smiling and smiling. 'You made the diagnosis.'

'You noticed the swab.'

'Together we make a great team.' Amy's eyes were bright with unshed tears. She was still holding Emma's hand but the little girl was slipping into a deep and natural sleep. 'Off you go. Tell her grandma and grandpa while I watch over her. And, Joss?'

'Yes?' He paused at the door and looked back.

'Thank you.'

'Think nothing of it.' His chest was expanding by the moment. The child would live, and it felt great! 'What else is a doctor for but to save lives? Given nursing staff with the power of observation you seem to have...well, as you say, we make a great team.'

He looked down at Amy and the child. They looked...magnificent. He closed the door behind him before she could see that his own eyes weren't exactly dry.

There were four people in Reception—Emma's grandparents, Joss's father and Daisy.

'We drove them here,' David told his son. 'And then we stayed. Did you really think we could go home before knowing the little one was safe?'

Joss looked at his father with affection. No. He didn't.

He operated with his heart, did his dad. It got him into all sorts of trouble. He'd buried three wives! His heart had been broken so many times, Joss thought, and each time he surfaced again to set himself up for more heartbreak.

Joss had never understood, but tonight, as he watched his father embrace his friends and celebrate this wonderful news—tonight he saw where his father was coming from.

Sure it hurt to give your heart. But now... This was such jubilation. Maybe...

Maybe what? What was he thinking of?

Was he thinking of giving his heart to Amy?

It wasn't wanted, he told himself savagely. Amy had a fiancé. She had a life. She had nothing to do with him.

'Can you put Mr and Mrs Crammond up for the night? Give them a bed?' he asked his father, but he knew before he answered what the response would be.

'Sure. But why?' The four elderly people were looking at him now with varying degrees of confusion.

'Emma ate something she shouldn't have,' he told them. 'You said she had roast meat and veggies and apple pie for dinner. Is that all? Did she eat anything that you didn't eat?'

Her grandparents were shaking their heads. 'No. She didn't.'

'And you're both feeling fine now?' They looked fine, he thought. Stressed but fine. Emma's illness had been dramatic. If they'd eaten the same thing they would have been ill by now.

'We're good.'

'Then I want you to stay that way. There's something that's contaminated Emma and until we know what it is I want you out of your kitchen. I don't want you to make so much as a cup of tea there before everything's tested. I'll ring Sergeant Packer and we'll go through the kitchen first thing in the morning.'

'She wouldn't...' Margy Crammond was becoming distressed. 'She wouldn't have eaten anything she shouldn't. Sergeant Packer... The police... You're not suggesting we poisoned her?'

'I'm doing no such thing.' Then, because it seemed the right thing to do—even though such a thing was unheard of in his professional life—he reached out and gave her a hug. 'Sergeant Packer's better at investigating than me. He's trained to figure out unusual circumstances, which is the only reason I suggested I'd call in his help. By tomorrow Emma should be up to answering questions and we'll sort out what happened in no time. But for now you should phone her parents and tell them she's fine. Then go to bed. And don't worry.'

He pulled back and lifted the old lady's face so she was forced to meet his smile. 'Can you do that?'

She nodded and gulped.

His father was watching with a strange expression on his face. 'Do you want Daisy and me to stay awake and watch them—just in case they're poisoned and it takes longer to take effect in adults?' Joss's father asked his question idly, as if it'd be no more than a mild inconvenience to stay up all night, and Joss thought, Yeah, he'd do that, too. He wore his heart on his sleeve did his father. He loved...

May Daisy live for ever. But if she didn't...

Loss wouldn't stop his father loving again, he thought. Loving was a part of the man he was.

And all of a sudden—for the first time in his life—he was jealous. Ever since his mother had died he'd thought his father was a fool to love. And here he himself was, being jealous.

He needed to go take a cold shower. He needed to go home. To bed.

In the room next to Amy. Yeah, right.

He took a deep breath.

'OK. We've had enough for tonight. Dad, don't worry about checking. If the Crammonds are sleeping in the same room they'll wake if either becomes ill, and I know they'll have enough sense to wake you. But if they had been poisoned by what they ate for dinner, they'd be ill by now. So relax. It's time for bed.'

They nodded and turned wearily away, but before David left, he gripped Joss's hand. 'Thanks, Joss,' he said softly. And then his grip hardened. 'I'm proud of you.'

CHAPTER SEVEN

THEY drove home in the wreckage-mobile. It had started raining again—hard—and Amy had to concentrate on the road. Maybe that was why they were silent for the entire journey.

Or maybe…maybe it was that Joss's life had subtly changed, and it occurred to him to wonder—had Amy's world changed, too?

No. The emotions that Joss was feeling were just that, he told himself savagely. *His* emotions. And stupid emotions they were at that.

They were silent because of what had just happened. They'd saved a life. A child's life. It felt good.

But it didn't override this strange new feeling that was flooding through him. Like life was opening up. It was a life he hadn't known existed or if he had, he'd thought it was stupid until now.

The world of loving.

They pulled into the garage. Bertram came lolloping out to greet them and Joss was relieved by the noisy welcome. He'd been trying to train the dog to be a bit more sedate, but tonight it eased the tension.

Why should there be tension? He and Amy were medical colleagues who'd just achieved a very satisfactory outcome. There shouldn't be any tension at all.

But…

'Goodnight, Joss. And thank you.' Before he knew what she was about she'd taken his face in her hands and she'd kissed him.

It was a feather kiss. A kiss of gratitude and goodnight.

There was no reason at all why he stood in the garage and stared stupidly after her as she disappeared into her house.

No reason at all.

Dawn saw them heading for the Crammonds' house.

'I'm coming, too,' Amy declared when Joss emerged from his bedroom. He'd rung Jeff the night before, emphasising that he didn't think this was a crime but that there was certainly something in the Crammond house that shouldn't be there. The Sergeant had suggested meeting at seven o'clock and Joss rose at six to find Amy bundled into jeans and a sloppy Joe sweater—looking absolutely delicious—and right into detective mode.

'OK. What should I take? A microscope? I don't have skeleton keys and I'm sure they're necessary.' She looked thoughtfully down at Bertram—who was looking thoughtfully up at her toast. 'Can we bring our sniffer dog?'

'He's not just a sniffer dog,' Joss told her, taking a piece of toast she'd prepared for him. Damn, why didn't toast taste this good when he made it himself? But somehow he made himself focus on Bertram. 'He's an eater dog. If he sniffed out poison he'd eat it straight away. He demolishes everything on the assumption that if it's not digestible he can bring it back up later.'

'That's an intelligent dog.' Bertram was promptly handed a piece of toast and he demonstrated his consumption ability forthwith. The toast disappeared with a gulp and he was wagging his tail for more. 'That's enough, Bertram. We have serious work to do. Do you think I should wear my raincoat with my collar turned up like they do in detective movies?'

'If movies were made in Iluka—yes, you should.' He stared out the window with morbid fascination at the sheets of rain pelting against the glass. 'I could be stuck here for months.'

'It suits me,' Amy said, but she'd turned back to the toaster and he couldn't see how serious she was. Or if she was serious at all.

*　　*　　*

The Crammonds' home was certainly not like a crime scene. It was the comfortable home of a cosy pair of grandparents and there was nothing suspicious at all.

Joss had been given the key the night before. Now the three of them, the policeman, Amy and Joss, pulled the kitchen apart.

'It'd help if we knew what we were looking for,' the policeman complained. 'You don't think they're into illicit substances—heroin or the like?'

'It crossed my mind last night,' Joss admitted. 'Not heroin, no. The symptoms of heroin overdose are very different to what happened to Emma. But I did wonder if they might be manufacturing amphetamines.'

'The Crammonds?' Amy's eyes widened in disbelief. 'You have to be kidding.'

'The strangest people are into drugs,' the policeman told her. He was inspecting canisters, one after another, poking his finger in and sniffing. 'One of our local grannies had a quarter of an acre of cannabis planted in her vegetable patch. I only found out about it when husband became fed up with her pulling out his tomatoes. They had a full-scale domestic, the neighbour got worried and I was called.'

'Here?' Amy shook her head in disbelief. 'In Iluka? Why did I never hear about it?'

'Because I sprayed the lot with weedkiller and told her to make a donation to the Salvation Army's drug rehabilitation programme,' Jeff said dourly. 'She was only growing it for herself—in fact, I suspect she hardly used the stuff and I didn't see much point in sending her to prison.'

'No.' Amy was still stunned.

'So Iluka's a hotbed of vice.' Joss was intrigued. 'I thought nothing ever happened in Iluka.'

'It's precisely because nothing ever happens that things do happen,' the policeman told him. 'People get bored.'

'Murder and mayhem?'

'You'd be surprised.'

'Yet you keep it under wraps.'

'If I can,' the policeman agreed. 'No sense in airing dirty linen in public.'

Amy was sifting through the cooking cupboard, peering into packages. 'So if they're into amphetamine production…'

'They'd need equipment and there's no sign of it. And they'd be nervous. The Crammonds weren't. They were quite happy to let us search the house and the garage.'

'Do we know what we're looking for?'

'No.'

'Great.'

But Joss was sorting through the clutter on the bench and he'd lifted the lid of the sugar bowl. Without really expecting anything, he'd taken a tiny pinch of sugar and placed it on his tongue. His face stilled.

'Jeff…'

'Mmm?' The policeman crossed to his side and peered into the bowl. 'What? It looks like normal sugar to me.'

'Taste it.'

'Yeah?' He did—though the look on his face said that he might as well be eating cyanide. 'Ugh. It's bitter. That's not sugar!'

'No.' Joss was gazing thoughtfully into the jar. 'It's not. They had apple pie and maybe Emma sprinkled it with what she thought was sugar. She might not have tasted it like that, and maybe her grandparents didn't use it.'

'But what is it?' Jeff was poking into the white substance with his finger. 'It's a bit finer than sugar but…well, you wouldn't notice it.'

'Where do they keep the packet?' Joss asked, and Amy poked around in the grocery cupboard under the bench until she found a half-empty sugar packet. She opened it and tasted.

'Sugar. It's fine.'

'Then what…?'

'What's nearby?' Joss knelt beside her—it felt good to

kneel beside her, he thought, and then gave himself a mental shake. He was losing his mind here. He should be concentrating on things that were important and all he could focus on was how good Amy smelled. Fresh and clean, and there was some lingering perfume about her. It was faint—as if it was in her soap, and not applied out of a bottle—but it was unmistakable. Lily of the valley? Gorgeous.

Groceries. Poison. Get a grip, Braden.

And there it was.

The packet was white with blue lettering. It was smaller than the sugar packet, and its lettering was clear.

Speedy Cure.

'What the heck is Speedy Cure?' he demanded, and rose, opening the packet as he did.

It was a white powder, slightly grainy. If you didn't know better, you could mistake it for sugar.

'What is it?'

'My mum used to use that,' the policeman told them, taking the packet away from Joss and staring down at it in recognition. 'It's used to cure corned meats. I seem to remember it makes a great corned silverside.'

'But what is it?'

The sergeant was turning over the packet.

'Sodium nitrate,' he read. 'Could that be it, Doc?'

'It certainly could.' Joss stared from the packet to the sugar bowl and back again. 'Maybe…if the sugar bowl was empty Mrs Crammond might have asked her granddaughter to fill it.'

'And if she said the sugar's in the cupboard…' Amy was way ahead of him. 'Emma would have grabbed the first package that looked like sugar.'

'Problem solved.' Joss grinned. 'How very satisfactory. And you won't have to arrest anyone, Jeff. Not that you would have, anyway.'

'I would have at this,' Jeff told them. 'If a child was hurt because of drug dealing…' He held up the packet and grimaced. 'Mind, they should have known better than to keep this where kiddies can get near it.'

'I think they'll have learned their lesson.'

'I'll go across to your dad's and tell them.' Jeff grinned at them both. 'Well done, the pair of you. You make a good team, you know.'

You make a good team...

It was a throwaway line. There was no reason for it to reverberate in Joss's head like a vow.

Amy was taking it lightly, which was just as well. 'We know we're a great team,' Amy said smugly. 'I'm thinking of talking to the weather bureau. Arranging it so that it keeps raining and Joss will have to stay.'

'Put in a word from me, too, then,' Jeff told them. 'If it meant we'd get a permanent doctor for this town then I'm all for it.'

'Why can't you get a doctor?'

'Are you kidding? Bowra has enough trouble keeping Doris, and she's impossible. There's no specialists this side of Blairglen—the place is a desert.'

'But it's a beautiful place to live.'

'Yeah. It is,' the policeman said dourly. 'But the only land without legal building caveats—bans on commercial building—is the land under the nursing home. The old man screwed up our lives when he set this place up and we were all too stupid to see it.'

There followed a horrid interlude with Emma's grandparents, who were overwhelmed with guilt.

'I asked her to fill the sugar bowl,' Margy Crammond sobbed. 'How could I have been so stupid? I hadn't realised how poisonous Speedy Cure is. Harold loves his corned beef and the general store only stocks the really basic meats...'

Here was another example of how isolated this place was, Joss thought grimly. The old man really did have a lot to answer for.

'With this population, surely there's a way you can get shops?'

'On what land?' Amy shook her head. 'No. He cheated a whole town of retirees out of a great place to live.'

'Hmm.'

The more he saw the more it intrigued him—and the more the girl by his side intrigued him. They drove back to the nursing home in silence, both deep in their thoughts.

'When are you and your Malcolm planning on getting married?' he asked as they pulled to a halt in the hospital car park. She looked at him, startled.

'What on earth…?'

'Does that have to do with me? Nothing.' He grinned with his engaging grin, which could get him anything he wanted. Almost. 'But I want to know. Are you waiting for six years?'

'Maybe.'

'How often do you see each other?'

'He comes every second weekend—except when there are floods.'

'Do you ever spend time at Bowra?'

'I can't leave Iluka.'

'The old man's will stipulated that you live here,' Joss objected. 'It didn't say you could never leave.'

'But with no doctor here…' She spread her hands in a gesture of helplessness. 'Mary and Sue-Ellen don't accept much responsibility and there are always crises.'

'What's the population here?'

'About two thousand.'

'And in the district?'

'You mean—once the bridge is rebuilt?'

'Yes. How many live in a twenty-mile radius?'

She thought about it. 'A lot,' she said at last. 'The farms here are small and close together—the rainfall's good and farmers can make a living on a small holding.'

'And all those farmers go to Bowra with their medical needs?'

'You're very curious.'

'Indulge me.'

She gave him an odd look—but what was the harm after all? 'They go to Blairglen mostly,' she told him. 'There's no specialists at Bowra—only Doris.'

'But Blairglen's more than a hundred kilometres away.'

'People travel. They must.'

She sounded odd, he thought. Strained. Well, maybe he'd asked for that. He'd kissed her. She was a perfectly respectable affianced woman. She had nothing to do with him—and he'd kissed her.

He'd really like to do it again.

Instead he sighed, climbed out of the car and walked around to help her out. She'd waited—as if she knew that he'd come and she welcomed the formality of what he intended. It was a strange little ritual and it had the effect of heightening the tension between them.

Help. When would the rain stop? When would they organise a ferry across the river? An escape route?

He needed it—because he wasn't at all sure what was happening here. Or maybe he was sure and he didn't know what the heck to do with it.

Their lives were worlds apart and that was the way they had to stay.

So somehow—*somehow*—Joss kept his hands to himself as she rose from the car and brushed past his body.

Amy was a practical, efficient, hardworking and committed nurse, he thought desperately. She wasn't wearing anything to entice. Right now she had on faded jeans, a soft cotton blouse and a pair of casual moccasins.

She was dressed for hard work. She was dressed in clothes so old no woman of his acquaintance would have been seen dead in them!

So why did he really badly want to…?

What?

He didn't know.

Or he did know. He just didn't want to admit it.

*   *   *

The Iluka nursing home was looking more and more like an acute hospital. It was busy, bustling and alive with a sense of urgency that had never been there before. Even the front of the nursing home had more cars than usual—this was the scene of the only action in Iluka and no one, it seemed, wanted to be left out. If they didn't have family here, the residents had friends—or maybe even just a sore toe, and maybe this charismatic young doctor could be persuaded...

This charismatic young doctor was feeling more and more out of his depth by the minute.

Bertram bounded out of the wreckage-mobile as the car drew to a halt in Amy's parking bay. They'd collected him on the way because of the residents' delight in him the day before, and he was greeted with even more pleasure than they were.

'Bertram.' Lionel Waveny's old face creased in delight as the dog appeared, and he put a hand proprietorially in his collar. 'Come with me, boy.' He was grinning like a school kid given a day off. 'Marigold's here,' he told them. 'She tells me she's probably got an overactive thyroid and she's sleeping in the room next to mine. She's feeling a lot better this morning but what she really needs is a visit from Bertram to cheer her up.'

'Go right ahead,' Joss told him, and Amy could only stare.

'I swear... Joss, yesterday that man could hardly remember his wife's name.'

'Dogs do that to people.' Joss looked at the old man's retreating back and Bertram's waving plume of a tail with satisfaction. 'Pet therapy. It's well documented. You want me to order you a dog or two as resident therapy?'

'You're kidding.'

'Just say the word.'

It was too much for her. Amy subsided into silence— which was just as well. They opened the doors to the sitting room and anything they said would have been drowned out straight away by baby screams. Ilona was being washed in preparation for her morning feed, and she was objecting in no uncertain terms to the violation of her small person.

The day took over.

Sue-Ellen greeted them as they walked in the door with a request for Joss to ring Emma's parents. To have their child so ill with no way of reaching her was making them feel desperate, and they wanted their daughter's progress given to them by a *real* doctor. Then Sue-Ellen handed over medical reports of all acute patients. All five of them.

This felt terrific, Amy thought contentedly as Joss read through Sue-Ellen's change-over notes. She stared around at the buzzing sitting room. Three of her oldies were helping bathe the baby and there were a couple more looking on with pleasure. One of those watching was Jock Barnaby. Jock had stared at the floor and nothing else since his wife had died two years ago!

Amazing!

What else? The knitting club—five ladies and one gentleman in their eighties—were trying to outdo each other by finishing the first matinée jacket. Through an open door she could see a couple of her inmates sitting by Emma's bed, just watching. Marie and Thelma were clucking over their pneumonia patient.

The place had come alive.

It could be like this all the time, she thought, dazed. It would be. If she had a doctor here. But how on earth could she ever attract anyone to practise here?

She couldn't. In a few days Joss would leave and it would go back to being same old, same old.

But meanwhile…she was going to soak it up for all she was worth, she decided. As she looked around her, her eyes danced with laughter and delight. 'This is great,' she said happily. 'Don't you think so, Dr Braden?'

'Just great,' he agreed weakly, and thought, Hell, it really is, but why?

Emma was recovering nicely.

Rhonda Coutts was looking good and her breathing had eased. Her pneumonia seemed to be settling.

Marigold's heart rate had settled after a good night's sleep. Joss needed a blood test to be sure, but he was more and more certain that his thyroid diagnosis was right. Marigold and Lionel had Bertram on her bed and the pair were petting and cooing over the big dog like first-time parents with their baby. Bertram was soaking it up with the air of a dog who'd found his nirvana.

This was a really strange ward round, Joss thought as he went from patient to patient, and it took an effort to keep his thoughts on medicine. He must—any of them could have a significant need that might be missed if he didn't treat this seriously—but with a nursing staff whose average age was about ninety it was a bit hard.

Amy didn't help. She couldn't disguise the fact that she loved what was happening around her, and her dancing eyes and bright laughter were enough to distract him all by themselves.

These people loved her. But she deserved better than to be stuck here for ever, Joss thought.

What did she deserve? A job in the city?

She'd do well in a city hospital, he decided. She was a magnificently skilled nurse, and she had the intelligence to be even more, given the right training. If she'd had the opportunity, she could be working alongside him as a fellow doctor, he thought, and the thought made him feel…odd.

All the thoughts he was having were odd. Stupid! It was increasingly obvious that by leaving her he'd be abandoning her.

It was no such thing, he reminded himself sharply. His life wasn't here. For heaven's sake, he couldn't set up medical practice in a town of geriatrics. He'd go nuts within a week.

As Amy was going nuts.

Amy had nothing to do with him.

He had one patient left to see—the new mother. By the time he reached Charlotte's room he was so confused he didn't know how to handle it, but somehow he put it aside. His examination of the young mother must be careful and thorough. Charlotte needed him. She was only one day post-op, and she was still suffering from her battering in the car crash.

'Talk to her by herself,' Amy said, leaving him at her bedroom door. 'She's traumatised and I don't know why. Maybe she'll be more willing to speak to you if you're alone.'

Amy was sensitive as well as competent, Joss thought, watching her retreating back.

She was a woman in a million.

She had nothing to do with him, he told himself for what was surely the twentieth time this morning. Concentrate on Charlotte!

Physically Charlotte was recovering well. His medical examination finished, he replaced the dressing over her wound and hauled over a chair to the bedside. Charlotte eyed him with caution as he sat.

'Hey, I'm not about to bite,' he told her, and she managed a smile.

'I didn't say—'

'No, but you looked.' He'd asked for her baby—Ilona— to be brought back into the room. Now he looked into the makeshift cot and smiled. 'Ilona's just right for a name. She's definitely beautiful.'

'Yes.'

'Does she have a surname?'

'I...I haven't decided yet.'

'Whether you'll use your name or her father's name?'

'That's right.'

'Are you going to tell me your surname?' Jeff had given him her surname but he wanted it to be the girl herself who gave it to him. The last thing he wanted was for her to think he'd instigated a police investigation.

She hesitated but Joss's hand came out and caught hers. 'I'm not sure what you're running from,' he said gently. 'But whatever it is, I'm not about to hand you over.'

'I'm not running.' She hesitated. 'My name…my name's Charlotte Brooke but… There's people I don't want to know…'

'That you're here?'

'That's right.'

'You need a bit of thinking time?'

'I do,' she said gratefully. 'I know it's messy, with medical insurance and things…'

'We can do all the paperwork when we discharge you,' he told her. 'That'll give you the time you need.'

'You won't tell Amy? Who I am?'

Joss frowned. Amy already knew but Charlotte's name had meant nothing to her. 'Is Amy one of the people you're hiding from?'

'No.' She bit her lip. 'But you won't tell her?'

'No.' But he was still frowning.

'I just want to do what's best.'

'Don't we all,' he managed. He was still holding her hand and now he looked down at the coverlet at her fingers. They were work-worn and there were traces of soil in her fingernails. She was used to hard physical labour. There was no ring on her finger. Nothing.

'Charlotte, if I can help…'

'You've done enough. You've given me my baby.'

'Amy did that.'

'That's what I mean.' Charlotte sighed and withdrew her hand. 'Before…it all seemed so easy. So possible. But now…'

'Now what?'

She turned away, wincing as the stitches caught. 'Now it just seems impossible,' she said.

'Did she tell you who she was?' Amy asked as he gently closed the door behind her. Joss had given Charlotte something to ease the pain and she should sleep until lunchtime.

'Yes.'

She caught his look and held. 'But she still doesn't want everyone to know?'

'Now how did you know that?'

'I'm a mind-reader.'

She was laughing at him. Her eyes were so disconcerting. They danced, he decided. She really did have the most extraordinary eyes.

'She told me who she was and she asked me to keep it to myself. I agreed. It means we can't bill her through Medicare until she allows us to, but she's agreed to let us use her name at the end of her stay.'

'It doesn't make any sense.'

'No.'

'But you agreed?'

'I agreed.'

She looked at him for a long moment. And then the smile returned to her eyes. 'You really are a very nice man, Joss Braden.'

It threw him. It was all he could do not to blush.

'I know,' he managed, and she grinned.

'And modest, too.'

'I can't deny it.'

'I've put you down as a fourth at bridge,' she told him, and that shut him up entirely.

'You haven't.'

'Someone had to do it,' she said demurely. 'My oldies tell me it takes brains to play bridge so who am I, a mere nurse, to take the place of a specialist?'

A mere nurse. She was no such thing.

She was enchanting.

'I was planning on…'

'Yes?' She fixed him with a challenging gaze. 'You were planning on what?'

'Doing more of my conference notes.'

'There's the whole afternoon to do that,' she told him. 'And tonight. And tomorrow morning and—'

'Whoa!'

'There's no urgency about this place,' she told him. 'Haven't you realised that yet?'

'Yes, but—'

'There you go, then.' She smiled her very nicest smile. 'Bridge, Dr Braden.' She pointed to the lounge. Looking through the glass door, he saw three old ladies clustered around a bridge table. Waiting.

When they saw him looking they smiled and waved.

'You've set me up.'

'Yep.' Her grin broadened. 'You've done your ward rounds and you're cadging board and lodging from yours truly. You have to pay some way.'

He had to pay.

The thought stayed in his mind while he learned the intricacies of bridge.

It stayed while he took Lionel and Bertram for a walk in the rain and listened to Lionel tell him a long and involved joke—four times. What was that joke about Alzheimer's? You can tell the same joke every time and get a laugh. You needn't bother getting fresh whodunits from the library—because you never remember whodunit. And you can tell the same joke every time and get a laugh.

Very funny.

He checked Marigold's heart and did some adjusting of the Lanoxin, checked on Rhonda's lungs, and that was it. It wasn't exactly intense medicine.

Amy was busy during the day but it was mostly administrative stuff. Organising meals on wheels. Sorting out the myriad problems of an aging community. She was wasted in this job, he thought. Her medical skills were far too good.

It wasn't worth saying that to her.

The whole set-up was a trap, he decide bitterly, and it was Amy who was trapped. He was here for a few days. Amy would marry her Malcolm and be here for life.

With no excitement at all.

Saturday rolled on. Joss found himself making kites with Lionel and wishing the weather would ease so he could try them out. They really were excellent kites.

He thought of what he'd be doing in Sydney now. He was a workaholic. Saturday afternoon he'd be coping with accident victim after accident victim, most of whom he never saw again after he left Theatre. The comparison with what he was doing now—keeping one old man happy by talking about kites and dogs—was almost ludicrous.

It was still medicine. He conceded that and wondered— how happy could he be in such a life?

He couldn't be happy. He needed acute medicine. He needed more doctors around him.

Iluka needed those things!

Amy didn't go home. Well, why should she? For once the nursing home was buzzing and vibrant and happy. Even with her new furniture, White-Breakers seemed dismal in comparison.

Bertram took himself for a run along the beach and came back soaked. Kitty stoked up the fire to a roaring blaze, and Bertram lay before the flames and steamed happily. Cook made marshmallows for afternoon tea and Amy helped the residents toast them in the flames. Thelma and Marie coaxed Joss into learning the basics of mah-jong.

If anyone had said a week ago that Joss could enjoy a day

like this he'd have said they were nuts. Now... He put down his tiles, ate his marshmallows, watched Amy's flushed face as she held the toasting fork to the flames and thought...

His world was tilting, and he didn't know how to right it again.

He wasn't even sure that he wanted to try.

David and Daisy came by at dinnertime and firmly took Joss home with them for the evening.

'You can't impose on Amy for every meal,' his father told him and Joss waited for Amy to demur—to say she really liked having him.

But she didn't.

She'd started to grow quieter as the afternoon had progressed. He'd look up to find her watching him, and her face seemed to be strained.

'Amy...'

'I can't keep you from your parents,' she told him. 'You have a house key to White-Breakers. I'm a bit tired after last night so I'll probably be asleep when you get home.'

Damn.

And when Joss woke the next morning she was already back at the nursing home.

'Have a good day writing your conference paper,' the note on the kitchen table told him. 'I'll ring if we need you but barring accidents you should have the day to yourself.'

Humph. He didn't want the day to himself.

He couldn't stay here. He was going nuts.

He drove to the nursing home—to see his patients, Joss told himself, but it was more than that and he knew it was.

He wanted to see Amy.

Sunday. The day stretched on, interminably, and wherever Joss went, Amy wasn't. Hell, how big was this home anyway?

The rain was easing, but the wind was still high. The talk was that as soon as the wind dropped they could get a ferry running. He could be out of here by tomorrow.

He might not see Amy again.

Why was she avoiding him?

Amy was going nuts.

Everywhere she tried to go there was Joss. He was larger than life, she decided, with his gorgeous smile and infectious laughter. He had the residents in a ripple of amusement, and she'd never seen them look so happy. Every single one of them seemed to have found a reason why they should be in the big living room.

She had a few residents who kept to themselves—who hated being in a nursing home and who showed it by keeping to their rooms.

Not now. Not when Joss and his big dog and his air of sheer excitement were around. With Joss here you had to think anything was possible. Something exciting might happen.

Exciting things didn't happen to Iluka, Amy thought drearily, and tried to imagine how she could sustain this air of contentment after Joss left.

She couldn't.

Exciting things didn't happen in Iluka.

But something exciting did.

'There's a boat hit the harbour wall.'

'What?' Amy had lifted the phone on the first ring and Sergeant Packer was snapping down the line at her.

'Of all the damned fool things, Amy. A speedboat tried to come in the harbour mouth—in this wind! It's come through the heads and nearly got in but it smashed into the middle island. Tom Conner was down there, trying to fish. There's someone in the water. Can you come?'

*   *   *

'Joss?'

'Yeah?' He was admiring Myrtle Rutherford's knitting and quietly going stir crazy. 'Trouble?' Amy's face said there must be—and it was serious.

'Possible drowning. Can you come?'

CHAPTER EIGHT

IT WAS as bad a situation as Joss could imagine.

The harbour entrance was formed by two lines of rock stretching out from the river mouth. In calm water boats could slip through with ease, but this wasn't a fishing port. It was a fair-weather harbour, maintained by the millionaires to house their magnificent yachts in the summer season. In winter the yachts were taken up to the calmer waters of Queensland where the élite could use them at their pleasure.

Now the harbour was empty, and with good reason. The rain had stopped but the wind was wild. Surf was breaking over the entrance. There were occasional clear gaps as waves receded but they were erratic. The rocks were jagged teeth waiting for the unwary, and what had come through…

It was certainly the unwary.

Jeff was there, and Tom Conner. The old fisherman and the policeman were identically distressed—and identically helpless.

'I've rung the Bowra coastguard,' Jeff told them. 'But it looks hopeless. We can't get a boat out there and it'll take a couple of hours to get a chopper here. If a chopper can operate in this wind…'

'Where…?' Amy was trying to see through the spray being blasted up by the wind. When she did she gasped in horror.

Right in the neck of the harbour was a tiny rocky outcrop. It formed a natural island, forcing boats to fork either right or left. Normally it was a darned nuisance but nothing more. If the harbour had been used for commercial fishing it might have been dynamited away but because this was a fair-weather harbour built for pleasure craft only, it wasn't worth the expense to remove it.

'It almost got through.' Tom Conner was literally wringing his hands. 'I saw him come and I was yelling, ''Damned fool, go back'' but he didn't hear. Then a wave picked him up and threw the boat like it was a bath toy. I still thought he was going to make it but the wave surged into the island and it hit hard and the guy was thrown out. He's still there.'

He was. Horribly, he was.

The boat was a splintered mess, half in and half out of the water. Its glossy red fibreglass hull was smashed into three or four pieces and as they watched it was being sucked down into the water.

There was a body on the rocks.

'He's been thrown further up,' Tom told them, and the old man was close to weeping. 'He hasn't moved.'

The man—whoever he was—looked like a limp rag doll. He was wearing yellow waterproofs and he was sprawled like a piece of debris across the rocks. While they watched, a wave smashed across the tiny island. The water surged almost up to his neck, shifting him, and they thought he'd slip.

He didn't. He must be wedged.

'Hell.' Joss said what they were all thinking. The island was about two hundred yards out. Impossible to reach him.

'He'll drown before the chopper reaches him,' Jeff said, and he sounded as sick as they all felt. 'That is, if he's not dead already.'

'Was he the only one on board?' Joss asked, his eyes not leaving the limp figure.

'Yeah,' Tom told him. 'The boat didn't have a cabin, and it was him doing the steering. I would have seen if there was someone else.'

Another wave crashed into the rocks and Amy's hand went to her mouth as the body shifted slightly in the wash. She felt sick. 'I can't bear this.'

'We need rope,' Joss said, and they all stared.

Jeff was the first to recover. He shook his head. 'Rope?

No way. You go in that water and you're a dead man. You can't swim against that current.'

'I'm not going in that water,' Joss snapped. 'How much rope can we find? I want a rubber dinghy and I want five hundred yards of rope—or more—and as many able-bodied people as we can find. Are there any families living within calling distance on the other side?'

'There's a few farms,' Jeff told him.

'Contact them and tell them I want as many people as possible on the opposite shore. Then I want Lionel and his biggest kite.'

'Lionel's kite…' Amy stared at him, seeing where his thoughts were headed. 'But…'

'But what?' His eyes met hers, challenging her to find objections.

She was starting to see what he was thinking. 'The wind's a south-easterly,' she said slowly. 'It'd take a kite straight across the river.' Her eyes widened. 'Maybe it could carry a rope. Maybe.' Despite the drama of the situation Amy felt a twinge of pleasure. Using Lionel's kites for such a plan… The old man would be delighted.

If it worked.

'Will a kite hold that weight?' Jeff sounded as if he thought the idea was crazy, but Amy was nodding.

'I bet it will. Lionel reckons a big box kite would hold a man, and in this wind…well, maybe the wind can work for us rather than against us.'

And at least it was a plan. It was something! Better than sitting waiting helplessly for the body to slip.

Jeff needed no more telling. Like them, he was desperate for action. Any action! He was already reaching for his phone.

'Great. Let's move.'

One thing Iluka was good at was mobilising. It was a small community. Most people were indoors because of the filthy weather. Jeff made one call to Chris and in ten minutes the telephonist had organised half the population of Iluka at the river mouth with enough rope to fence a small European country. Plus there were three rubber dinghies, one enormous box kite—Lionel attached—and ten or so men and women standing on the other side of the river.

'How much weight can that kite hold?' Joss demanded, and Lionel scratched his chin and looked upward. There wasn't a trace of his dementia.

'In this wind? As much rope as you like. I reckon it could lift me.'

'That's what I'm counting on,' Joss told him, and he managed a grin. 'No, Lionel, I'm not planning to sky-ride on your kite. But I'm depending on it just the same.'

There was a delay of a few minutes while ropes were securely knotted together—a delay where all eyes were on the prone figure sprawled on the island rocks. Maybe he was already dead. Maybe this wasn't worthwhile.

But... 'I think I saw him move.' Someone had brought binoculars and Amy was focussing on the yellow waterproofs. 'I think his hand moved.' She couldn't see his face. She could see very little but a mass of yellow.

It was enough. 'Then we try,' Joss told her. He'd been deep in discussion with Lionel. Lionel had shed his years like magic and was talking to him as an equal.

Amy was still confused. 'I don't know how...'

'Just watch. Lionel and I have it under control.' He hesitated and then conceded a doubt. 'I think.'

The kite was launched. In this weather it was dead easy. Lionel and a couple of his mates simply held it to the wind and it lifted like magic, its huge trail of rope acting as if it were a piece of string. It soared skyward, a dozen men feeding the rope out. Lionel held a lighter string, as if he needed to anchor it to himself.

They needed a stronger anchor than Lionel. They'd fastened the end of the heavy rope to rocks—just in case the men couldn't hold it. In weather like this they could end up with the kite sailing on to Sydney.

'How do we get it down?' Amy asked.

But Joss and Lionel had the operation under control. The kite was over the river now, sailing past the heads of the crowd gathered on the other side. Lionel motioned to the lighter cord he was holding—a cord that on closer inspection turned out to be a loop. 'We tug hard on this and she collapses,' he said diffidently. 'Watch.'

They watched. He pulled the cord and the fastening on the kite came unclipped. The box kite soared upward—next stop Queensland—and the snake of rope and the looping cord crumpled across the river, the ends coiling downward to be seized by the people on the opposite bank.

They had a rope bridge now, with men and women on either end pulling it tight.

'With teams holding the rope over the island, I reckon I can reach him,' Joss told them. At Amy's horrified look he shook his head. 'I'm not swinging Tarzan style. I might be brave but I'm not stupid. Lionel and I worked it out. I fasten the dinghy using a slider that moves along with me. I loop a slider around my belt and I fasten the dinghy to me. The lighter cord Lionel was holding forms a loop so we can use it as a pulley, with the teams at both ends controlling as I work myself along the heavier rope. Easy. When I reach the rocks I haul whoever he is into the dinghy. I take a couple more ropes with me to make him safe on the way and Bob's your uncle.'

Amy was just plain horrified. 'And if you fall in?'

'I told you,' he said patiently. 'I'm attached to the rope and I'm attached to the dinghy. If worst comes to worst I can come back hand over hand—but if it's all the same to you I'll stay in the dinghy.'

'If it's all the same to me, you'll stay here.'

'And let him drown? I can't do that.' He stared into her

appalled eyes, and something passed between them. Something.

That something was deeper than words. He put out a hand and lifted her chin, forcing her eyes to meet his. Their gazes locked for a long, long moment. Someone was looping a rope through Joss's belt but he had eyes only for Amy.

'I'll be fine.'

'You'd better be.' Her voice was choked with emotion and he thought, What the hell—if he was going to be a hero, surely he was allowed to kiss a fair maiden?

In truth he didn't feel all that brave.

But he was here. The body on the rocks was about to be swept out to sea. The average age of those around him was about seventy or maybe older—even the policeman was over sixty—so he was the youngest man there by almost thirty years.

And he knew damned well that if he didn't go then it'd be Amy who roped herself to the dinghy. She was accustomed to taking the weight of the world on her shoulders.

This time it would be him. If this was all he could do for her—then so be it.

He had no choice.

He bent and he kissed her, a swift demanding kiss that was more about grounding himself, somehow, making sense of what he was about to do.

A month ago, maybe he would have thought what he intended was madness—risking himself for someone who might even now be dead. But Amy was watching him with eyes that shone. Amy was holding him. Amy's mouth was pliant and soft under his and she knew what he was doing. She might hate it but she expected it because he knew without doubt that if he didn't go then she would.

Amy, who gave her all.

He...loved her?

Now was not the time for such crazy thinking. Now was the time to put her away from him and loop the rope at his waist around the massive rope that now swung across the river.

They were waiting for him.

'Let's go,' he said. He gently put his hands on Amy's shoulders and put her away from him. It was like a physical wrench.

As it was for Amy. She lifted her hand and touched his cheek—one fleeting touch—and then stood back.

Her life had been about hard choices and she knew more than most that Joss didn't have a choice at all.

He had to go.

There was nothing for her to do but watch.

The dinghy was fastened to the stronger cable so it couldn't be pulled off course, and they'd attached the dinghy to the looping lighter line so those on either side could pull. Joss, therefore, had only to keep his little craft stable.

It was easier said than done. The water was a maelstrom of surging surf. He lay back in the boat to give him maximum stability, his hands holding the thicker cable as he was pulled carefully, inch by inch, across the river. Each time a breaker surged he stopped and concentrated on keeping the boat upright. It was a mammoth task.

A couple of times the breakers almost submerged the boat but Joss emerged every time. He'd done his preparation well. The two teams had control of the boat as much as they could, and Joss was attached to the boat and to the cable. He had the best chance…

He just had to keep upright.

Amy's heart was in her mouth. There wasn't a word from the team on her side. Joss's father was here—he was head of the team feeding out rope after the dinghy, helping to guide it. Daisy was in the team holding the main cable. Margy and Harry Crammond were here, and with a shock Amy recognised at least eight inmates from her nursing home.

They might be old but when there was work to be done they weren't backward in coming forward.

They were her people.

She loved them so much. She looked out to where Joss was fighting the waves and the impossibility of what she was thinking broke over her yet again. She was falling in love—no, she'd fallen in love—but her choice was bleak indeed.

No. She had no choice. Her place was here, with her people. Joss belonged to another place. Not Iluka.

He was not her man.

But…dear God, she loved him.

All Joss could think of was staying afloat. Of staying alive. But he wasn't alone.

The teams on either side were manoeuvring his boat, trying as best they could to keep it steady as they inched it toward the island. He was alone, but not alone.

They had another dinghy and he didn't need to be told that if he fell someone else would try.

Maybe Amy…

No! He had to reach the island.

Somehow he did. The dinghy reached the island just as the waves had backed off. Those holding the ropes had timed it brilliantly. He unfastened himself—even that was hard—and stepped out onto solid rock. The boat was immediately dragged away. For a moment he panicked—but only for a moment. Of course. They'd drag it away from the rocks to keep it from being punctured. Another wave broke and he had to kneel and cling to keep a foothold.

As the wave receded, he looked up. The figure was still sprawled face down on the rocks. As Joss scrambled to reach him, he stirred and moaned.

He was alive!

Just. He'd come close to drowning, Joss guessed. His eyes were glazed and not focussing. He was barely conscious.

Joss worked fast. The guy was trying to breathe but it was shallow and laboured. Was the airway clear? Carefully he manoeuvred the injured man onto his side, conscious all the time of the damage he could do himself. It was no use making the man's breathing easier if he destabilised a fractured neck in the process.

Another wave surged but the man's head was just above the water line. Joss moved his own body to take the brunt of the wave's force. The guy muttered and groaned again.

'You're OK, mate,' he told him. 'Just relax.'

There was no response.

The man was about Joss's age, he guessed—in his early thirties, maybe? He was dressed in waterproofs but his clothes underneath were neat and almost prim. He wore a white shirt and smart casual trousers—or they had been smart. They were smart no longer.

This was no fisherman.

Of course it wasn't a fisherman. A fisherman would have known it was crazy to take a boat out on a day like today.

With Joss's body deflecting the water from his face, the man's breathing was deeper, his colour returning. Joss took a quick blood pressure and pulse reading—blood pressure ninety, heart rate a hundred and twenty.

Why the low blood pressure? Was he bleeding?

He'd groaned. He must be close to surfacing. What else?

Swiftly Joss ran his hands over his patient's body, doing a fast physical examination. There seemed little to find on his upper body. He'd copped a blow to his head—there was a haematoma already turning an angry red-purple on his forehead but it didn't look too bad. The bone structure seemed intact. If there were fractures, they were minor.

His hands moved lower. The guy's waterproof pants had been ripped and his knee was bleeding sluggishly. He lifted the leg and a gush of blood met his hand from below.

Hell.

With the man's breathing stable, this was a priority.

Joss grabbed a pressure bandage, pushed it down hard until the bleeding eased and then taped it into position, but the pool under the man's leg was bright with blood. He must have lost litres.

There was nothing he could do about it here. The waves were still surging over him. He had to get the man back into the dinghy but he was trying to assess if anything else needed urgent attention before he did.

One leg seemed shorter than the other.

Joss frowned and did a visual measurement, but it wasn't his imagination. He was sure.

The hip was either fractured or dislocated—or both. The blow to the leg must have shoved the femur out of position. Joss flinched again as he saw it.

He had to move fast. Dislocated hips were a time bomb. The muscular capsule, the lining inside the cup holding the major bone to the leg, should provide blood to the ball of the thigh joint. Disrupt that for too long and the head of the femur would begin to die. He had a couple of hours at most.

He couldn't do anything about it here. He needed help. An orthopaedic surgeon? An anaesthetist?

Amy.

He'd make do with what he could get and Amy was a darned sight better than nothing. He glanced toward the shore and he could see her. She had on a pale blue raincoat and she was staring at him through the spray...

Amy. It was enough to give a man strength to move on to the next thing.

These rocks were sharp! They were stabbing into him as he knelt.

He needed to get them both out of here.

He moved back to the guy's head. He was breathing in fast, jagged rasps. His eyes were starting to open, confusion and pain making him struggle.

Joss held him still. 'It's OK. You're fine.'

Well, sort of fine. But it seemed a good thing to say, as much to reassure himself as his patient.

And maybe it was the right thing to say. The guy's eyes opened a bit more, as if the light hurt at first, and then they widened.

'What...?'

'You've had a spot of an accident,' Joss told him. *A spot.* There was an understatement. 'Your boat hit a rock.'

'Who...?'

'I'm Joss Braden. I'm the doctor at Iluka.'

'I'm Malcolm,' the guy said. His eyes widened and Joss saw agony behind them before he passed out.

Malcolm?

Amy's Malcolm?

Maybe he'd been desperate to see his love, Joss thought, but as he looked down at the guy he knew that it didn't make sense.

He'd passed out from the pain, he thought. His breathing was easier now. It'd be his leg...

If you were measuring pain levels, dislocated thighs would take you off the scale. If he regained consciousness he'd be a basket case.

Once more he checked the guy's breathing and then he signalled to the teams to bring in the boat.

This was the hardest part of all, but it had to be done now. If Malcolm had been conscious he'd have been screaming in agony. He had to try while the guy was out of it. Waiting wasn't going to make this easier.

Swiftly he tied a rope, harness fashion, around Malcolm's chest and shoulders, then attached it to the cable that the teams had manoeuvred above his head. It meant if Malcolm was to fall from the dinghy he'd be swinging head up from the cable until somehow Joss could haul him in again. Joss flinched at the thought of it. Maybe it wasn't satisfactory— there was an understatement again—but it was the best he could do.

Then he had to drag the inert man into the dinghy—which was probably the hardest thing he'd done in his life. The term dead weight meant something, and Malcolm was just that. A dead weight. Joss slipped a couple of times, crashing into the rocks as he hauled Malcolm into the water. He'd hurt his own leg, he thought grimly, feeling the warmth of his blood dripping down his sodden leg.

But finally he had Malcolm in the bottom of the dinghy, and he was pushing the craft away from the rocks while the guys with the cables pulled him outward.

He was still thinking, his hectic brain in overdrive. Maybe he could signal them to haul the dinghy to the mainland side of the river. That side meant expert help. An ambulance ride to Blairglen and specialist orthopaedic surgeons, who were what this guy needed.

But on that side lay a reach of jagged rocks, both submerged and out of the water. The men on the mainland side were having trouble holding the cable free of the rocks. He didn't like their chances of getting the boat over them.

On the Iluka side the breakwater rose steeply out of deep water. It was much, much safer.

So…back to his prison?

Back to Amy.

Fine. He held up his hand to signal that he was ready to go, and they started to pull.

It was a nightmarish journey but somehow he did it. With Malcolm crumpled in the base of the dinghy Joss somehow kept the boat stable as the men on the bank hauled him in. Often the breakers surged over the boat. Each time he had to lean over and make sure Malcolm was still breathing. He hadn't gone to all this trouble to let him drown!

Finally the dinghy was nearing the rock face of the harbour wall. There were men clambering down the rocks. Eager hands were reaching out to hold the boat steady—old hands, but willing.

And Amy.

'Joss,' she said as she took his hand and helped haul him up onto the safety of the rocks. She held him for just a fraction of a second too long. A fraction of a second that said she'd been scared out of her wits.

He held her, too—to draw comfort and give it.

Amy. His home...

But she was already turning away to look at the man in the bottom of the dinghy. They were lifting him up the rock wall, using the dinghy as a stretcher, and her eyes widened in stunned amazement as she saw who it was.

'*Malcolm?*'

There was no time for questions.

'I want him back at the nursing home—fast,' Joss snapped as he helped haul the boat up the rocks. 'I need to get the hip X-rayed. What's the story with the helicopter?'

'The wind's too fierce to bring the chopper in. The forecast is for it to ease. Maybe in a couple of hours...'

'That's too long. Amy, I probably need to operate. Can you...?'

She took a deep breath.

'Of course I can.'

'Amy...' Malcolm was drifting in a pain-induced haze but as they loaded him into the back of Jeff's police van he seemed to focus. Joss had administered morphine but with that hip the pain would still be fierce.

'Malcolm.' Amy took his hand and Joss was aware of a stab of...what? Jealousy? Surely not. He had nothing to be jealous of. This guy was Amy's fiancé. He had every right to hold her hand. Even if he had the brain of a smallish newt.

'What on earth were you doing out in the speedboat?' Amy asked.

And Joss thought, Maybe she's thinking the same thing. Brain of a newt. The thought gave him perverse satisfaction.

Malcolm was struggling to speak. 'Wanted to see…' he whispered, and closed his eyes.

'I'm here.' She stroked back the wet strands of his blond hair. The man was seriously good-looking, Joss decided— not entirely dispassionately.

He ought to be. If Amy loved him.

'Hush,' she was saying. 'Just relax. We've given you something to help the pain.'

'My leg…'

'It'll be fine. Don't try and fight it. Close your eyes and see if you can sleep.'

Malcolm seemed to think about that for a while as Jeff eased the van onto the main road. Then his eyes widened and he stirred, fighting the fog of pain and morphine and shock.

'I crashed my boat.'

'Mmm.' Amy was still holding him.

'What…what are you doing here?'

'You're in Iluka,' she told him. 'You tried to bring the boat into the harbour. Can you remember?'

He frowned in concentration. 'I wanted… I wanted to see…'

'It doesn't matter now,' Amy told him, wiping a trace of blood from his forehead. 'You've hurt your leg and we need to fix it. Just lie back and relax and we'll get you to sleep.'

Moving back into medical mode was a relief. Joss was more confused than he cared to admit. It must have been the danger of the whole thing, he decided, but he was having trouble concentrating on what needed to be done. It was a relief to pull up at the hospital.

No. It wasn't a hospital. It was a nursing home, he reminded himself, but the way it was going they'd need to apply for twenty beds of acute care. Maternity, orthopaedics, kids' ward—take your pick.

Iluka Base Hospital. It had a good ring to it.

It had a crazy ring. He was trying to think about something
other than the way Malcolm's hand was gripping Amy's.

He was losing his mind!

CHAPTER NINE

ONCE back at the nursing home they concentrated on medical matters—much to Joss's relief. He could function as a doctor. It was this interpersonal stuff that he couldn't handle.

It was the way he felt about Amy!

The inmates of the nursing home were back in medical mode as well, and Joss looked at his crazy medical team and saw that they were really enjoying this. The drama had lifted them all out of themselves. Maybe next week they'd go back to being senior citizens but for now they were needed and useful, and they'd never been happier. They helped Malcolm out of the police van with the same expertise as they'd unloaded Charlotte two days ago.

Marie even put a detaining hand on Joss's arm and said, 'Doctor, you're dripping blood. You come with me and I'll dress it before you start looking after anyone else.'

Bemused by the old lady's starched efficiency, he let her apply a fast dressing—enough to stop blood staining the carpet—and then he followed Amy to where she'd organised X-rays.

This place was running like a well-oiled machine and he thought, What a waste for it to turn back into a nursing home... For now, however, it was an acute-care hospital and he could treat it as such. He turned his attention to the X-rays.

Much to Joss's relief, the contusion on Malcolm's forehead didn't match a skull fracture. The skull was fine. There was only the hip. Which was bad enough.

To Joss's huge relief there was little bone damage. The force of the impact on the rocks had punched Malcolm's femur out of the rim of the cup, but the cup itself was intact.

143

There'd be nerve damage, Joss thought as he studied Amy's pictures. The sciatic nerve would be traumatised and that could well mean months of pain before it resettled. But for now there was only the matter of getting the femur back in place before the hip was irretrievably damaged.

'Can we organise helicopter evacuation?'

'Kitty checked while you were doing your hero stuff,' Amy told him. 'The weather reports are saying the wind's dying and the rain has cleared. The place where they've landed before is deep mud but Jeff's organising gravel to be laid now. It should be possible to bring in a machine by this evening.'

'Not until this evening?' He winced, staring at the X-ray. 'This won't wait.'

'Can you do it?'

'With your help. Are you willing to do the anaesthetic?' It wasn't fair to ask her but he must.

Her gaze was untroubled. 'Yes. It has to be easier than Charlotte. Doesn't it?'

He gave her a faint grin of reassurance. 'Yes, it does. But contact the helicopter people and tell them we do need an evacuation, even if it's late. With a hip dislocation there may well be nerve damage. He'll need specialist assessment for long-term care. But the first thing to do is get the ball back into the socket. I'll ring the orthopod at Sydney Central and run this by him, but I think he'll tell me what I'm already guessing. This can't wait until this evening. We need to do it now.'

Amy gave the relaxant anaesthetic almost without guidance. She was getting to be an expert, she thought grimly. Joss was setting himself up for the procedure ahead and, while Malcolm slipped under the anaesthetic, she had a moment to think.

What on earth was Malcolm doing here? This was so out of character for him that it was crazy.

It didn't make sense—but a moment's thought was all she had. Joss was ready.

'We'll administer suxamethonium as well,' he told her. They'd stripped off their outer gear and scrubbed, but there was time for no more. 'The muscle will have seized up as the hip wrenched out of place.'

Mary was in Theatre as well this time, so he had two trained nurses—or rather, two trained nurses under eighty, with Marie and Thelma still acting as back-up. Mary was beginning to think she'd missed out on the excitement of Charlotte and if there was any more excitement to be had she'd like a hand in it, too, please. From nurses who'd been willing for Amy to shoulder total responsibility, she and Sue-Ellen were now both actively looking for ways to help.

The hospital was seeming more and more an acute-care facility and all the staff were stepping up a notch in their expectations of themselves.

Amy could only be grateful. Her hand might be rock steady as she administered the anaesthetic, but inside she was jelly.

This was Malcolm.

Or…maybe it wasn't just that. Maybe part of it was re-action. To watching Joss haul himself up those damned rocks. To seeing the water wash over him…

'Ready?' Joss asked and she took a deep breath.

'Ready.'

In the end it was fast. Joss had done this once before as a surgical registrar, but he'd done it then under supervision. It wasn't the same as doing it alone. More than anything, he wanted a skilled orthopaedic surgeon to be present—but it was himself or no one.

What was the old adage? See one, do one, teach one? If that was the case, he'd be ready for a teaching job tomorrow. With that wry thought he started.

The moment the muscle relaxant took hold, Joss placed his

knee up on the table to give him greater leverage. Once in position he took hold of Malcolm's upper thigh. While the two nurses watched in astonishment—this wasn't like any surgery they'd ever seen—he lifted his other knee until he was kneeling completely on the table. Now he was gripping Malcolm's right leg, the lower leg at ninety degrees to the upper.

This didn't look like any operating scene you'd see in the movies, Amy thought, stunned. This was a real manipulative nightmare, where what was called for was a mixture of brute strength and skill. And courage.

'Can you lean in and push down on each side of the upper pelvis?' Joss demanded. He was breathing hard—what he was attempting took as much strength as skill, and it wasn't a job for weaklings. He needed Amy to do this. In truth, he needed another strong male, but once again Amy was the best that he had.

'Here?'

'Yes. Right. Both hands flat and push as hard as you can. Mary, take over the monitor for a moment. Right, Amy. Now!'

She pushed. Joss pulled, smoothly but sharply and with all his force.

The joint slid back with a sound somewhere between a dull pop and the clunk of two pieces of wet timber being knocked together.

The thing was done.

'Fantastic,' Joss said. He climbed off the table, found a chair and put his head between his knees. And stayed there.

Amy stitched Malcolm's leg—and then she stitched Joss.

'Because the doctor's leg really needs stitches, Amy,' Marie had started scolding the minute they came out of Theatre. 'If you don't do it,' the old nurse added, 'then I will, and my eyesight's not all that good.'

So while Mary supervised a recovering Malcolm, Amy

took Joss into her office, closed the door and demanded he remove his still damp clothes. When he demurred she simply pushed him into a chair and removed his trousers for him. Plus the rest of his wet clothes. She handed him a hospital gown and barely waited for him to be respectable before she hauled off Marie's makeshift dressing over the gash on his leg.

'I'm a grown woman,' she told him. 'Plus I've been a trained nurse for years. There's nothing I haven't seen so let's get on with it. Modesty's for sissies.'

'I'm not—'

'Moving. No, you're not. If you try, I'll fetch half a dozen senior persons and we'll tie you down.'

'Amy…'

'Shut up and let me do what has to be done.'

It was a jagged tear, not so deep as to be serious but ragged enough to definitely need stitches. Joss sat on the day-bed in her office while she applied local anaesthetic, cleaned and debrided the edges and then set herself to the task of sewing him up.

It was a weird sensation, Joss decided as he sat and let her suture. It was a sensation of being completely out of control.

It was a feeling to which he was growing more and more accustomed.

'What do you reckon Malcolm was trying to do?' he asked, more to keep his mind off what she was doing than anything else. He could feel her pulling his skin together but it wasn't the feel of her stitches that was the problem. It was the feel of her, period. Her touch against his skin. The way her braid fell forward over her shoulder while she worked. The way those two little concentration lines appeared on the bridge of her nose and her tongue came out—just a peek. She was concentrating.

She was gorgeous!

Yeah, right. The lady might be gorgeous but she had a

fiancé who was recovering in the next room. Her fiancé was a man who'd risked his life to see her.

Dopey git!

And Amy's words echoed his thoughts.

'It does seem a little over the top.'

He agreed entirely. 'Even Romeo wouldn't have been so daft.'

She thought about that and applied a couple more stitches. 'Romeo was pretty daft.'

That pleased him. He wasn't quite sure why, but it did. 'You mean your own personal Romeo's act of devotion doesn't meet with your unqualified approval.'

'He could have picked up the telephone and called with much less dramatic effect.'

'Where's the romance in that?'

'The rain's almost stopped and the forecast is for decent weather at last. The ferry may well be up and running by tomorrow. Surely he could have waited.'

'So you're going to be…how sympathetic?'

Amy thought about it. 'I guess I'd better be a bit sympathetic. Though if he thinks I can help with the repayments on a splintered speedboat…'

'It was his speedboat?'

'Yeah, but he only uses it on the river. I've never known him to take it out to sea. It just doesn't make sense.'

'He must be missing you enormously.'

'And that doesn't make sense at all.'

'Why not? Isn't the man in love?'

She thought about that. She looked like a sparrow, Joss thought, with her head to one side, thinking while concentrating at the same time. She was using tiny stitches—this would be the prettiest scar known to man.

He'd be able to look at it and remember Amy…

And that was truly ridiculous.

'I guess he must be,' she said, and he had to think about what he'd asked. Right. Isn't Malcolm in love?

Of course. He had to be.

But Amy was still considering. 'It's so out of character.'

'He's not prone to over-the-top declarations of passion?'

'He's sensible.'

'Well, what he did today wasn't sensible in the least.' He felt peeved, he thought, and he couldn't figure out why. She'd tied off the last stitch and had lifted a dressing from the tray. 'Leave this,' he told her. 'I'll do it.'

'I—'

'You go back to Malcolm,' he said, and if he still sounded peevish he couldn't help it. 'He needs you.'

'Nope.' She had herself back in hand. 'I'll dress this and then I'm putting you to bed.'

'Pardon?'

'You're having a sleep.'

'I am not.'

'You've risked life and limb, your leg's sore, you've got half a dozen nasty bruises that I can see, and if I peered closer I bet I'd see more.'

'You would not.' He hauled his hospital gown closer.

'And don't tell me you didn't nearly pass out in Theatre.'

'I didn't.'

'Marie, Mary and I all reckon you did. That's three against one. And we hold the ace.'

'I beg your pardon.'

She swooped and lifted the bundle of still damp clothes from where he'd dropped them. 'I'll take these to the laundry, so if you're going anywhere you go in your hospital gown. And I'd check the mirror for your view from behind before you take that option. You'd be shocked to the core! Meanwhile…'

'Meanwhile?' He sounded stunned. He *felt* stunned.

'Meanwhile, we've put Malcolm in the bedroom at the end of the hall. It's a double room with a spare bed. You take yourself down there and get between the covers. Marie's asked Cook to make you an omelette and a cup of tea and then the order is to sleep for the rest of the afternoon.'

He was eyeing her cautiously. She was one bossy woman and he was a man who didn't like to be bossed. By anybody.

But this was Amy and she was laughing at him, and he was...

Damn, she was right. He was shell-shocked. He'd thought it was just his emotions but it was more than that. He tried to stand but his legs felt distinctly odd.

Maybe he quite liked to be bossed.

Maybe the order was changing.

'You've had enough,' she said, and she moved to support him. His arm came around her and he held on.

He held on for too damned long—but neither wanted to let go.

This was crazy. She was engaged!

'I'll go,' he said at last.

'You'd better,' she whispered, and they both knew what she meant by that.

He'd better—or they weren't prepared for the conse-quences.

Lunch—or maybe it was dinner, it was halfway between the two—was great, but by the time he'd finished eating his head was heavy on his shoulders and he was prepared to concede that Amy knew what she was talking about.

Mary was watching over Malcolm, who lay in the bed beside him. Damn, why wasn't it Amy? It wasn't and he had to be content with Mary clearing his plate and tucking him in. Like he was a four-year-old.

'Now, you sleep,' she said sternly—and, like it or not, he slept.

When he woke it was dark and someone was in the room.

For a moment he was confused, trying to remember where he was. The room was in darkness. A nightlight was shining from under the bedhead, and he could just make out someone framed in the doorway.

A woman?

Charlotte.

What was Charlotte doing here?

He opened his mouth to speak but her whisper cut across the room. This must be what had woken him.

'Malcolm?' It was an urgent whisper and brought a whisper in response.

'Charlotte.'

Charlotte glanced at Joss but he didn't stir. As far as she was concerned, he was one of the several old men in the nursing home, settled down early for his routine bedtime.

Joss wasn't settled at all. *Charlotte knew Malcolm?*

The plot thickened...

He fixed his eyes firmly shut, told himself to ignore the itch on the end of his nose—itches only seemed to happen when you had to be still—and strained to listen.

'Are you OK?' She was shuffling forward. She'd only been out of bed a couple of times since the Caesarean and her stitches would be pulling. She moved awkwardly forward with another nervous glance toward Joss.

Joss tried an obliging snore and wuffled a bit, like he was eighty.

'No.' That was Malcolm from the next bed and Joss could hear the pain in his voice. 'I'm not OK. Hell, it hurts. I damn near killed myself. Of all the...'

'Why did you come?'

'I had to see you, of course. I wanted to make sure you didn't tell...'

'Didn't tell Amy?' Charlotte's voice broke on a sob. 'Of course. I was stupid to think you must want to see me.'

'I did.' Joss could hear him making an effort to placate her and he could imagine the man putting a hand out to touch the woman as she reached his side. They were so close...

He could just reach out and tweak the curtains...

The curtains around the beds gave an illusion of privacy. Behind them the two could imagine they were alone. As they did. Maybe Malcolm didn't know he was here, and Charlotte believed that he was asleep.

'I wanted you so much,' she was saying.

'So I came.'

'You almost killed yourself.'

'Yeah, I was a fool. But I wanted to see our daughter.'

'Not a fool. Oh, Malcolm…'

Yeah, he's a fool, Joss felt like saying, but he showed great forbearance and didn't. Sheesh, the weather was easing! The ferry could be up and running by morning. He'd needed to see his daughter, so he'd risked her being fatherless?

He'd risked Joss being lifeless!

And… *Malcolm was the baby's father?*

But something else was bothering Malcolm. 'You didn't tell Amy?' The guy was in deep pain, Joss thought, listening to his voice. He should pull back the curtain and check his obs and give him pain relief.

Not yet.

'I didn't tell Amy,' she repeated dully. 'I wanted to. That was why I came here in the first place. I was sitting outside her house, waiting for her to come home. I knew, you see. I asked at the post office and they said she knocked off at two and came home for a couple of hours. I'd come too early so I had to wait, because I wasn't brave enough to come here. Only then I went into labour and panicked and tried to drive home. And I crashed. Then…when I was here and Amy was so nice…I couldn't tell her. I tried to but I couldn't. I'd thought…if I could only get her alone, I could explain.'

'Explain what?'

'That we're in love,' Charlotte whispered. 'That I was carrying your baby. That we want to marry.'

'But we don't want to marry. We can't. Not yet.' It was an urgent demand. Charlotte must have completely forgotten that there was someone in this bed—or else she didn't care—and Malcolm surely hadn't realised.

'Of course we want to marry. You have a daughter. Surely you want to acknowledge her. And you don't love Amy.' She was verging on hysterics.

'Charlotte, remember our plans. I'm engaged to Amy and it'd be stupid to break it off. I'm all she has.'

'But you love me.'

'I can't break off the engagement with Amy. You must see... That's why I came the way I did. I thought no one would be at the harbour mouth in this weather. I'd park the boat by the old moorings and come in when Amy wasn't around. Sunday afternoon there's always so many old folk visiting I wouldn't be noticed. I could avoid the staff and just ask one of the oldies where you were. I had to stop you from being stupid.'

'Stupid—to tell her we're in love?'

'Charlotte, no.' The intensity was too much for Malcolm, Joss thought. He could hear the desperation in the man's voice. He should get up and stop this—tell Charlotte that Malcolm was in no state for visitors.

He did no such thing. Not yet. He waited.

'It's the money,' Charlotte said flatly, and Joss heard Malcolm draw in his breath. The money. Of course. 'You still think she'll marry you and then you'll get a share of all the money she inherits. That's why you panicked and rode that damned speedboat into the rocks. You didn't trust me to be quiet. When you rang last night and I was so upset... I might have known you'd do something stupid.'

'You weren't being logical last night,' he told her wearily. 'You weren't making sense. Charlotte, this is all about our future. Our baby's future. Amy's worth a fortune and if I marry her, if I support her for the time she's trapped in Iluka... Charlotte, it'll set us up for life. Even if I only get my hands on ten per cent of what she's worth, it'll be enough. It's only at weekends. You know she can't leave Iluka.

During the week we can be together, like we always have been.'

'And our baby?'

It was too much. Malcolm gave a grunt of sheer exhaustion. 'Charlotte, I can't think. Not now… Please.'

It was time for the physician to call, Joss decided. He might be riveted to this conversation but he didn't want Malcolm to collapse.

The sciatic nerve was a hell of a nerve to insult. Malcolm would be in pain for months, and Joss thought it couldn't happen to a nicer person. He took a deep breath, rose and twitched back the curtain.

They stared at him in the dim light. He must look quite a sight, he thought. Surgeon in hospital gown, having slept off the effects of coming close to drowning.

They didn't look too flash themselves. They might be as old as he was but they looked for all the world like two silly kids in trouble.

Malcolm closed his eyes—he didn't know who Joss was and his body language said that he didn't much care. Joss gave him a searching look and rang the bell. OK, the man had treated Amy like dirt but he needed morphine.

'I'll get you something to ease the pain,' he told Malcolm, and then he looked at Charlotte. Charlotte knew who he was, and he could tell by her dawning horror that she'd figured he'd heard everything that had happened.

His argument wasn't with Charlotte. She was as much a victim here as Amy was. Maybe more.

'You need to go back to bed,' he told her gently. And then, as Amy appeared at the door and looked in bewilderment from Joss to Charlotte to Malcolm and finally back to Joss, he said, 'Amy, here's Charlotte ready to go back to bed. Can you bring me ten milligrams of morphine for Malcolm? Then maybe you could go and tuck Charlotte in. She has something to tell you.'

Then, as Malcolm jerked into awareness and started to speak, he held up his hand.

'Leave it,' he told Malcolm. 'You've done enough damage as it is. I risked my life saving you and now I'm not sure why. For now, Charlotte has a choice. She tells Amy what I've just overheard—or I do it for her.'

The helicopter arrived an hour later to collect Malcolm. It landed on a newly gravelled patch at the back of the golf course, the rain had miraculously stopped, the wind had eased back to moderate and the landing was easy.

Iluka was back in touch with civilisation.

'You can go, too,' Amy told Joss. It was a subdued Amy who'd returned from seeing Charlotte to hand him a pile of cleaned and dried clothes. She'd said nothing—just shaken her head in mute misery at his enquiry. Now she returned to his bedroom to find him fully dressed and looking down at a sleeping Malcolm. 'If you want to go back to Sydney you can go with him.'

If he wanted to go…

He gazed across the bed at Amy and he thought, Why the hell would he want to go to Sydney?

Why not?

'Um…my dog's here. I can't leave Bertram.'

'We can take care of Bertram until you have time to come back and collect him. If you like, I'll have someone drive out and collect your belongings from White-Breakers.' She glanced at her watch. 'Jeff's bringing the helicopter team here now to prepare Malcolm for the flight. They're paramedics, so you're not needed on the flight, but if you want to go…' She took a deep breath. 'If you want to go, then decide now.'

He thought about it for another two seconds. 'No.'

'No?'

'Let Charlotte take my place.'

'Charlotte wants to stay here.'

'Does she?'

'She's one mixed-up lady,' Amy whispered. 'Just like me.'

'Do you feel like kicking this louse?' he asked curiously, and she thought about it.

'No,' she said after a long time. 'For one thing, he's already kicked himself harder than I ever could. For another…' She hesitated. 'He's not so bad.'

'He two-timed you.'

'Yes, but…'

'But what?'

'But maybe I would have gone mad without him.' She looked up at Joss and her eyes were bleak. 'You think that sounds soft. Maybe it is. But four years ago, when I knew I had to come back here, I felt I was living in a nightmare. Malcolm was my friend. He coped with all the paperwork— he made it possible for this place to be built—he was here for me.'

'He was here for Charlotte as well.'

'No, that came later.' She sighed. 'Charlotte is very…honest. She's explained everything to me. She met Malcolm a couple of years back and they started a friendship—which turned into a relationship. After all, what Malcolm had with me was a weekend once a fortnight.'

'And the promise of a fortune.'

'Maybe.' She was watching Malcolm's face. He was deeply asleep, his chest rising and falling in a regular rhythm, his body sleeping off the battering shock it had received. 'Charlotte said that wasn't the only reason he wanted to keep the engagement going. Why he wanted to marry me. She said he was worried about me.'

'And you believe that?'

'Maybe I do.' She met his look, and her eyes were challenging. 'Maybe I need to.'

'Why?'

'Because he was all I had.' She swallowed. 'He was a future. A husband. Babies. A semblance of normality.'

'You're not thinking of still going through with it?' he demanded, and she shook her head.

'Of course not. Charlotte's had his baby. Regardless of what Malcolm wants, as far as I'm concerned our relationship is over.' She tugged at the engagement ring on her third finger until it came off. Then she stood staring down at the diamond glistening in her palm. 'The helicopter's here,' she said bleakly. 'You can go. You can all go.'

'Do you love him?' Joss asked, watching her bleak face.

'I…'

'Amy?'

'Leave it,' she whispered and turned and walked out the door.

Should he go to Sydney?

Joss rang Jeff who said, yes, the chopper was here, the machine could fit four passengers and they were prepared to take him as well as Malcolm. He was bringing the van to the hospital now to collect anyone who wanted to go.

Could he be ready himself?

No.

Malcolm was as ready as he ever would be. Joss wrote up a patient history ready for handover and then walked out to the living room.

Lionel was there, cutting a vast ream of yellow fabric into kite pieces. He'd lost his favourite kite and another one had to be made pronto to take its place. Heaven forbid that there ever be spare space in the living room!

'More kites?'

'There are never enough kites,' Lionel told him, and Joss nodded in full agreement. No. There were never enough kites. He looked around at the jumble of crazy constructions that Amy put up with and he wondered how many nursing-home managers would have allowed it.

There were never enough kites.

There was never enough…joy?

'You should sell them,' Joss said, more for something to say than anything else. 'You make great kites. You could make some money from them.'

'Not here I couldn't,' Lionel said morosely. 'When I retired I thought I'd set up a little shop here and sell them to kids coming to the beach. That's a joke. Even if kids came—which they don't—the only place I could sell them now is from the nursing home. Who comes to a nursing home looking for a kite?'

'Why could you sell them from a nursing home and nowhere else?' Joss said slowly, thinking it through. Lionel was a bit confused. Was this just another example of his confusion? 'Why not out of your garage?'

But Lionel wasn't confused about this. 'There are caveats on every other damned place,' he said. 'There's one quarter-acre block zoned for commercial use for the post office and general store and that's it. The rest of the district is zoned purely residential to perpetuity and use for commercial purposes is banned. Except this place. But I can't see me sticking up "Kites for Sale" above the nursing-home sign. Can you?'

'I guess not,' Joss said, but his brain was beginning to tick over.

An idea was stirring at the back of his mind. It probably wouldn't have a hope of working. There probably wasn't a loophole.

But if he was right…well, why not?

Did she still love Malcolm? That was the last unanswered question.

The helicopter team arrived and together they organised Malcolm for the long flight to Sydney. Joss helped immobilise his leg, administered more painkiller and sedative to help him with the flight and then stood back as Malcolm said his farewell to Amy. Charlotte was nowhere to be seen.

'I'm sorry, Amy,' Malcolm told her as they lifted his stretcher into the police van. He took her hand and she submitted to his urgent grip. 'Listen, Charlotte and I...' He was speaking urgently. 'I don't...'

'You don't have to tell me that what's between us is over.' She smiled down at him and there was the trace of affection in her voice. 'You needn't bother. I know. It *is* over.'

'Charlotte wants to stay here.'

She was deliberately misunderstanding what he was trying to say. 'That's OK. We'll look after her for you.'

The conversation wasn't going the way Malcolm had planned but his head was too fuzzy to do anything about it.

'Amy...'

'I'll give your engagement ring to your father,' she told him. 'I'd give it to you now but it may get lost. Or would you like me to give it straight to Charlotte?'

'No! Amy!'

But she was shaking her head and she even had a rueful smile on her face. 'Maybe you're right. That would be bad taste. Almost as bad taste as fathering a child while you're engaged to someone else.' She hesitated and then stooped and kissed him lightly on the forehead.

'Goodbye, Malcolm,' she said and stood back to let him go.

She was...crying?

Joss turned to find there were tears welling in Amy's eyes.

Damn the man. He was so angry he felt like following the van, stopping it and dislocating the other hip.

Had he been mistaken in telling her about Malcolm's infidelity? Or in forcing Charlotte to tell her?

He thought about it. Maybe Malcolm could have convinced Charlotte to keep quiet. Maybe Amy would still have married him, had a couple of kids, been happy with her weekend husband until her six years were done.

What else was there for her?

Anything, he thought angrily. There had to be a life for

this woman—a life that she wanted rather than the one dictated by the despotic old fool, her stepfather.

He scowled at the retreating back of the police van and then looked up to find Amy watching him.

'Why didn't you go when you had the chance?' she asked. 'You could have escaped.'

Was that what he wanted? To escape? He thought about it and looked at her pale face and thought about it some more.

'I talked to Jeff,' he told her at last. 'He reckons if the rain doesn't start again they'll have a ferry lined up by tomorrow. Bertram and I can drive out of here under our own steam.'

Her face closed in pain—but he wasn't sure. Was it pain for him—or pain for Malcolm?

Maybe even she didn't know.

'Bully for you,' she said, and turned and walked into the nursing home without another word.

CHAPTER TEN

Joss popped in to check on Charlotte before he went home, and found her weeping into her pillows.

'He's just weak,' she sobbed. 'I didn't see it before. But he's a fool. Thinking I'd do something to ruin our future, dashing here in his stupid speedboat in this weather, thinking Amy wouldn't find out...' She took a deep breath. 'You know, I really did think he was doing this for Amy's sake. I thought he was committed, and it was too late for him to draw back. I was even sympathetic. But now... I just don't know any more. *And I loved that speedboat as much as he did!*'

Whew! It seemed Malcolm had blotted his copybook in more ways than one. If Malcolm wanted a long-term relationship with this lady, he had a few bridges to build, Joss decided. As it was, he'd gone from having a relationship with two women to being very close to having a relationship with neither.

Amy was looking as bleak as Charlotte.

They drove home in the dark together but there seemed little to say. There was a constraint between them that was growing worse all the time.

He should have kept his oar out of her affairs. She was looking like she'd lost her world.

What was it with the creep? What did Malcolm have that Joss didn't?

The thought brought him up sharply. For heaven's sake, was he jealous?

Jealous of a guy with two relationships?

No. He was jealous of a guy who'd had Amy's heart in the palm of his hand.

His leg hurt. All of him hurt. All of him ached, and it wasn't just physical. He ached for Amy. He ached for the impossibility of the whole damned set-up.

He ached.

Back at the house, Bertram greeted them with the joy of one who'd been abandoned for at least a month.

He needed a run.

'I'll take him to the beach,' Amy told him. 'You put yourself to bed. Your leg must hurt.'

It didn't hurt so much any more. Not if it meant not going to the beach with Amy.

This was his last night here. Tomorrow the ferry would be operating and he'd be out of here.

'I'll come.'

'Your leg…'

'My leg can drop off for all I care. I'll come.'

So they walked, slowly in deference to Joss's stitched leg. He'd have gone faster but she deliberately held back. She was wearing faded jeans and a big sloppy sweater. Some time during the day her braid had started to work free and she hadn't had time to rebraid it. She looked like part of the landscape, he thought. A sea witch. Lifting her face to the sea. Drinking it in.

She looked free.

She was anything but free.

The dog ran in crazy circles around them, the circles growing larger and larger as he revelled in this, his last night on the beach. Tomorrow Bertram would be back in his hospital apartment, Joss thought ruefully, limited to two long runs a day. After the freedom of the seashore it'd seem like a prison.

Sydney would seem like a prison.

He put a hand down and suddenly Amy's hand was in his. It was almost an unconscious gesture on his part—to take her hand—but when he'd done it, it felt good.

It felt great!

She felt like his woman.

She loved Malcolm?

'He's a rat,' he growled, and he felt rather than saw her surprise.

'I know.'

'You won't take him back.'

'No. I won't take him back.' She was speaking as if from a distance—as if speaking to herself. 'I never should have got engaged to him in the first place.'

'Why not?'

'Because I didn't love him.'

There. The thing had been said. It was out in the open, to be faced by the pair of them.

'But still you agreed to marry him,' he said cautiously and she nodded. She kicked a ball of sand before her and it shattered into a thousand grains and blew away on the wind. The weather was clearing by the moment. Joss was wearing her father's overcoat but he hardly needed it.

The moonlight was on their faces. The salt spray was gentle. It was their night.

'I just can't handle it,' she said tightly. 'I know I'm doing a great job here, I'm keeping all these people happy. Just…what about me? That was why I got engaged to Malcolm. So I could have a life—any life—apart from the nursing home.' She kicked another lump of sand but this time it didn't dislodge and she almost tripped. 'Damn,' she said, and he knew she wasn't speaking about the sand.

'Take me out to your rock,' he said on impulse, and she hesitated. 'Go on.' His hand was still in hers. 'It's my last night here.'

'It's my special place.'

'Share it with me.'

'You don't want…'

But he was propelling her forward. 'I want.'

'You'll get your feet wet.'

'Heroes don't mind wet feet,' he told her. 'Not when in pursuit of fair maidens.'

She stared at him for a long, long moment, and then, without a word, she turned and led him out across the rocks.

And when they reached it, he turned her and took her firmly into his arms.

There were so many things between them. There were so many obstacles. But for now, for this moment, they fell away as if they didn't exist.

The dangers, the pain and the confusion slipped away. Joss held Amy in his arms and once again the thought flooded his mind. This was his woman. Here was his home.

She smelled like the sea. His lips were on her hair and the sea spray was a fine mist, damp against his mouth. Her figure was a lovely curving softness against his chest. The fabric of her ancient sweater was as lovely as silk to him. He gloried in the softness against his hands as he felt the pliant contours of her body, and he felt his body surge in recognition of a longing he hardly recognised.

He'd wanted women before, he thought, wondering, but not like this.

She was his.

She had to be his. His need was so strong it was almost primeval, a surge of something as old as man itself. Here was his mate. Half of his whole. He held her tighter, savouring the moment, waiting for her face to turn up to him as he knew it must, for her lips to find his...

Waiting to claim her.

This was impossible. She was a captive in this place. She couldn't leave, and he couldn't stay.

But how could he leave her? All this time he'd been fighting against a commitment he didn't understand. He'd thought his father a fool for allowing himself to love, but love wasn't something you chose.

Love was here.

Love was now.

She was pulling back—just a little—just enough to see his face in the moonlight. What she saw seemed to satisfy her.

'Joss,' she said, and it was enough.

His mouth lowered to hers and he claimed her.

His woman.

And Amy...

This was an impossibility. This man... He had no place in her life. She was trapped here and tomorrow he'd be gone.

But tonight...

Tonight she held him close. She was twenty-eight years old, she'd been engaged to someone else for the last two years, it was six years before she could leave this place...

All of those things were as nothing on this night.

For tonight there was only Joss.

'I love you,' she whispered against his chest, so low that Joss could hardly hear against the sound of wind and waves. It didn't matter. She didn't want him to hear. It wasn't a declaration to him. It was a declaration to herself.

Tomorrow the loss and the loneliness would begin. Tonight there was Joss.

She lifted her face to his and she linked her hands behind his head and pulled him down to her.

'Joss,' she whispered, and after that she couldn't whisper a thing. For a very long time.

Afterwards, Joss could never remember how they made it to the house. Making love on the beach wasn't an option. Maybe in midsummer—but not when the sand was still soaked from two weeks of storms and the wind was still chill. No. He wanted this woman in the comfort of a bed.

Liar. If the bed wasn't on offer...

He wanted this woman any way he could have her. And he wanted her for ever.

She wasn't arguing. In that final moment as she placed her

lips against his they both knew that they were surrendering themselves to each other. Completely. If this night was all they had, then so be it. Better one night than never. If this night was to last a lifetime then they'd take this night with joy.

They weren't protected. Joss had nothing and when he remembered he groaned, but Amy wasn't fussed at all.

'If you're happy to take the risk then so am I,' she murmured as they reached the bedroom door and paused. There was a brief moment of sanity to reassure Bertram—and lock him in the kitchen—and take stock of what they knew lay ahead. 'If I end up pregnant from this night I'd think it nothing but wonderful.' She smiled up at him. 'And you?'

He thought about that. *Nothing but wonderful...*

Amy carrying his child?

So much for his fear of commitment. The thought filled him with unadulterated joy.

'You're sure, my love?'

'I'm sure. I'd make a very good single mum.'

He had his own ideas about that. Single mum? Humph!

But now wasn't the time to declare his hand. Not until he was sure. If she thought she was headed for single parenthood, well and good. For now.

With a whoop of sheer loving triumph he swept her up into his arms so he was carrying her down the hall. He was laughing into her gorgeous dancing eyes and she was laughing back at him, loving him, wanting him...

'Then so be it,' he told her. 'So be it, my love. Let's see if we can make a baby. The way I feel tonight, we might even make quads!'

They were falling onto his bed, their clothes were disappearing. The moonlight was slanting across their bodies, as if in blessing...

Man and woman, becoming one.

*   *   *

Dawn came too soon. Or maybe it wasn't dawn. Something was ringing.

Joss stirred. Amy was cradled in his arms, her lovely hair was splayed out over his chest and she was cradled against him in love and in peace.

Who said married couples needed double beds? he thought sleepily. Single worked just fine.

'Um…it's the telephone.' Amy lifted her head. 'Why did we end up in your room when the phone's in my room?'

'The world's in the rest of the house. Here there's just us.'

Which was fine—but the telephone was ringing.

'Maybe it's urgent,' Joss said.

'I think we should forget the medical imperatives. Charles the First can give it a shot.'

Charles the First? Oh, right. The ancient doctor with dementia. 'Maybe.' But the ringing kept on. 'Maybe someone's dead.'

'There's not a lot we can do if they're dead,' she said practically. 'Call the undertaker—not us.'

'Amy…'

She sighed. 'Hey, I'm the conscientious one, not you.' She rubbed her face against his bare chest, and her hair felt like silk against his skin. The sensation was unbearably erotic. 'OK, oh, noble doctor. Go and answer the phone. I'll keep the bed warm.'

'Promise?'

She smiled down into his eyes, love and laughter fighting for supremacy. Love won. 'I promise.' But she was kissing him so deeply that he couldn't resist.

The phone stopped. Two minutes later it started again and Joss swore.

'It's nine o'clock on a Monday morning,' Amy told him, still laughing. 'The world has a right to intrude.'

'It's not nine o'clock.'

'That's what your watch says.'

'You're lying on my watch.'

'That's not all I'm lying on. Go and answer the phone.'

'Did I tell you I love you?'

She beamed. 'Yes. But tell me again if you like.'

'I love you.'

'There you go, then.' She kissed him lightly on the lips and pushed him away. 'That makes a hundred and eleven. But tell me again.'

'I love you.'

'A hundred and twelve. Go and answer the phone.'

It was Sue-Ellen from the nursing home.

'The ferry's operating. Emma's parents were the first over and they want to know if they can take their daughter home right away.'

Joss groaned. He really did need to check the child first.

'I'll be there as soon as I can,' he told her.

When he returned to his bedroom Amy was gone.

'Amy?'

'I'm in the shower.'

'You promised to keep the bed warm.'

'I lied. People do.'

He thought about that as he hauled open the bathroom door to find her under a cloud of steam.

'I don't,' he told her.

'Yeah, right.'

There was only one way to handle insubordination like that. Joss hauled the shower screen wide and swept Amy up into his arms. They stood naked as the water poured over them and he kissed her so hard she lost her breath and had to pummel him away with her fists. Breathless and laughing, she leaned back in his arms and looked up at him with love.

'If you need to see Emma before she's discharged, we need to go.'

Damnably they did.

'Joss...'

'Mmm?'

'Thank you for last night.'

'It's the first of—'

'No.' The laughter died then. 'Joss, it's not the first of anything. It's a one-off. Today you'll get into your step-mother's amazing pink Volkswagen and you'll drive onto the ferry and out of my life.'

'No.'

'Yes.' She struggled to be free and reluctantly he loosed her. Not so much as you'd notice, though. She was still linked within the circle of his arms.

'I've had a long-term engagement,' she told him. 'I don't want another.'

'But—'

'No.' She was holding him close but her voice was urgent. 'Joss, you know I can't leave here for six years. This place would die. So many people would lose so much. I can't hurt them and you wouldn't want me to.'

He thought about that. In truth, he'd been thinking of little else. Except for how wonderful this woman was.

How he needed to keep her.

'You can't stay here,' she told him.

He thought about that.

'Joss?'

'Mmm?'

'You need to return to Sydney.'

He did. Damnably, he did. There was so much to do.

'Remember me,' she told him. 'But not...not with faith-fulness. I'm not waiting for you and you're not waiting for me. We're free.'

Free.

Once it had seemed the only way to be. Now, as he kissed

her one last long time, it seemed a fate worse than any he could think of.

Free?

Where was the joy in that?

They made their way back to the nursing home in almost as deep a silence as the way they'd driven home the previous night.

So much had changed—and yet so little. They reached the nursing home and they were surrounded by need.

Emma's parents were waiting to see him, desperate to know her poisoning hadn't caused long-term damage. Charlotte's father had appeared, wanting to blast someone for his daughter's unhappiness, Rhonda Coutts's daughter had come to make sure her mother was being well cared for and was recovering. And more…

There must have been a longer queue on the far side of the river waiting to come to Iluka than the queue on the Iluka side waiting to get out, Joss decided. He fielded one query after another, always conscious that Amy was working close by. Amy was here.

Amy would always be here.

'Now the ferry's operating, Daisy's happy for you to take her car back to Sydney,' his father told him, and he had to raise a smile to thank her. Driving a pink Volkswagen would get him a few odd looks but those looks were the least of his problems. 'That is,' his father added, looking sideways at his son, 'if you still want to go.'

He didn't, but it was never going to get easier. Another night like last night and it'd be impossible.

His life was waiting in Sydney. Or…the chance of a new life?

'He's going.' Unnoticed, Amy had come up behind them. She smiled at David, who'd driven in to the nursing home specifically to find his son. 'He's being kicked out of his lodgings, so he must.'

That was news to Joss. 'I'm being kicked out?'

'Yes.' Her face was strained and pale but somehow she summoned a smile. 'It's far too crowded with two people, one dog and only ten bedrooms. Someone has to go. I drew straws and Joss is it.'

'Will you keep Bertram?' Joss demanded suddenly. He couldn't bear to think of her in that mausoleum alone. But she shook her head.

'Of course not. He's your dog.'

'I'll buy you a pup.'

'Thank you, but no.'

And into his head came a faintly remembered line. 'I want no more of you...' Where had that come from? Schoolboy Shakespeare? Wherever, it was apt.

It was time to go. He couldn't commit himself to this woman. At least...not yet.

He still had almost a week of leave left. He could stop at Bowra and then...

'You look like you're aching to get back to Sydney already,' David said, watching Joss's face. He smiled at Amy and explained. 'Joss always gets this far-away look when he's making plans, and he's making plans now. What's on back in Sydney?'

'I'm not sure,' Joss said slowly. 'I won't know until I get there.'

There was one more heartbreaking moment as Joss stood in front of the little Volkswagen ready to leave. Bertram was sticking his head out the window and wagging his tail in anticipation, waiting for Joss to say goodbye.

This was no aching farewell of two star-crossed lovers. Star-crossed lovers didn't get a look-in at Iluka, where everyone's life was everyone's business.

David and Daisy were there, plus almost every nursing-home patient and close to every Iluka resident as well. In these few short days Joss had won Iluka's heart.

As they'd won his heart. He could see why Amy couldn't leave.

'Come back soon,' they called, and he looked at Amy's ashen face and thought not.

Not until some of those plans came to fruition.

CHAPTER ELEVEN

JOSS spent the first night in Bowra. First there was a long appointment with Henry, Malcolm's father. To his relief Henry was no Malcolm. The old lawyer was intelligent and interested, and once he learned what Joss intended he couldn't do enough to help.

'God knows, that woman has suffered enough,' the old man told him. 'When I think of how my stupid son has treated her... And now there's Charlotte, of all women. I know Charlotte—she's the daughter of friends of mine. How the hell he managed to keep their relationship secret...

'By the way, you needn't worry about Charlotte,' the old man added grimly. 'I'll see to it that Malcolm marries the girl if that's what she wants. And if she decides not to—and who could blame her? Well, Malcolm will provide for her anyway. He'll do it if I personally have to cut off his inheritance to see it done.'

'I think we've had enough of inheritances,' Joss told him, and the old man agreed.

'Well, let's sit down and see what can be done about this one. This idea of yours... I never thought— It'll take courage.'

'More than courage,' Joss told him. 'But do you think it can be done?'

Then there was a meeting with Doris, the Bowra doctor, who greeted him at first with suspicion and in the end with excitement.

'If you can pull it off...'

Another person wishing him joy.

*   *   *

His father was working on the Iluka council members, and as Joss left Bowra and headed for Sydney he rang David on his cellphone, pulling over to the side of the road to take the call.

'Here are the figures you asked for,' his father told him. 'Hell, Joss, it looks good. It looks great.'

'And the bridge?'

'We reckon we can do it.'

Now there was only the medical side to contend with, Joss thought as he steered the Volkswagen back onto the road. And the bank.

And the government authorities.

Only.

It was a month before Joss returned. He'd hoped it would be sooner but his plans had been extensive. No half-measures would do and he wanted to be sure.

Now he was as sure as he could be. The old lawyer in Bowra was chuckling to himself in huge delight. Amy's stepfather would be turning in his grave, he decreed, and he couldn't think of a better fate for the man.

Joss's father had taken the train to Sydney and was following behind in the pink Volkswagen. Joss was driving something better.

The rebuilding of the bridge hadn't been started yet—they still needed to use the ferry—but once the work started Amy would guess what the plan was and he wanted to be the one who did the telling. He was as sure as he could be that they could pull this thing off. It was time she was told.

So Joss put his brand-new Range Rover—with a strange new sign on the driver's door—on the ferry, and then drove it around the cliffs where he'd crashed a month before and pulled up outside the Iluka nursing home. Bertram was out of the car the moment he opened the door, flying in to find all the friends he'd made on their last visit.

Joss followed.

Amy was in her office. She heard the twittering from the living room, she heard the mah-jong set clatter as it hit the floor, and then the big red dog burst into her office. He came bounding up to greet her, his paws landed on her shoulders and she darned near fell over.

Bertram!

David will have brought him back from Sydney, she told herself, fighting down the sudden surge of stupid hope. David and Daisy had told her they were going to Sydney to collect the Volkswagen. What could be more sensible than them bringing the dog back home for a visit?

Joss wouldn't be here.

She glanced out the window to see a gleaming new Range Rover parked at the entrance. It had a sign on the door. ILUKA HEALTH RESORT.

It didn't make sense.

But before she could fully take it in, Joss was standing in the doorway. He had an absurd expression of hope on his face, like he was Bertram and he wasn't sure whether he'd be kicked or hugged.

'Joss…'

Her voice faltered. She'd made such resolutions. He'd come back to visit his father occasionally, she'd told herself, and she had to greet him as a friend. Nothing more.

But he was still looking at her, his expression was just the same and it was too much. She was across the room and hugging him, kissing and being kissed, welcoming him with all the love in her heart. 'Oh, Joss.'

'Amy.' He was beaming and beaming, putting her away from him so he could take her all in. 'You haven't changed a bit.'

'You've only been away for a month.'

'I thought you might be pregnant.' There was a gasp behind them and Joss's beam widened. 'Hi, Kitty.'

'H-Hi.' The secretary rose on feet that were decidedly unsteady. She was choking on laughter. 'Pregnant, huh?'

'I am not,' Amy told him indignantly. 'After one night— what do you think you are?'

'You reckon it'll take more than a night? What a good thing I'm back.'

'Joss…'

'I'll leave you to it, shall I?' Kitty managed, and sidled out of the door. She very carefully didn't close the door behind her.

'Amy.' Joss kissed her again and from outside the door there was a collective sigh. Iluka's residents *en masse*.

'Um…' Somehow she pushed him away.

'Um?' He was smiling down at her, with the smile that had the capacity to make her heart do handsprings all on its own. 'Is that all you can think of to say?'

But she was recovering, just. Friends. She had to greet him as a friend. What she was feeling was the way of insanity.

'Joss, I can't…'

'You can't what?'

'Love you.' There. The thing was said. She waited for him to take it on board and step back.

He did no such thing.

'You can't love me?'

'No.'

'But the future I've planned is founded on just that.'

'What?'

'The fact that you love me.' He looked deeply concerned. 'Are you sure you can't? If you try very hard?'

'Joss…' She was torn between tears and laughter. It was so good to see him again. It was wonderful.

'Maybe you can just pretend,' he told her. 'You see, I don't think I can stay here as Medical Director of Iluka Health Services if I don't have a wife to support me. A man of such importance needs a wife.' He was grinning at her like a fool. 'All those opening ceremonies, all that ribbon-cutting—a man needs a wife, if only to hold his handbag.'

'You,' she said slowly, 'are being ridiculous.'

'Nope. I'm proposing.' He delved into a back pocket and produced a tiny crimson box. He flipped the lid and there lay the most beautiful ring she'd ever seen. A band of gold held a magnificent central diamond, twinkling and sparkling in the morning sun coming in from the window by the sea, and a host of tiny sapphires surrounding it.

'Oh, Joss.' It took her breath away.

'Do you like it?'

'It's…it's beautiful,' she told him, and he grinned.

'Yep. And it's bigger than Malcolm's.'

She looked up at him then and gasped in indignation. 'Of all the—'

'Wonderful men?'

'Conceited, arrogant—'

'Wonderful men,' he repeated, and lifted the ring from the box. 'Can I put it on your finger?'

But she hung back. 'Joss, you must see that I can't.'

'No.' His smile faded and he took her arms in his and held them. His eyes were on hers, and what was in his eyes made her catch her breath. Love and care and trust.

Love…

'Amy, I've organised us a life. If you'll listen.'

She thought about it. She'd give him the benefit of the doubt, she thought. She'd indulge herself as well as him. Pretend for a few short minutes that they had a future.

But Joss had released her. He crossed to the door and flipped it open and there were no fewer than fifteen faces and one dog crammed into the doorway. Grinning, he took a folder from his father and closed the door—but not completely. The fifteen noses would have been squashed. Then he marched over to the desk.

'This,' he said, unfolding a huge blueprint onto a desk, 'is the plan for our future.'

Amy stared at him. Then she stared at the plan.

And gasped.

It was a map of the bluff—the tract of land that held the nursing home. The nursing home took up about five per cent of the available land. But now...

The plan included the nursing home but much more. There was a hospital, about twice the size of the nursing home. There were a score of houses dotting a park-like setting and overlooking the sea. There was a row of shops—more than a dozen with places earmarked for more—plans for a cinema, an indoor heated pool, a remedial health centre, doctors' surgeries. A hotel named 'Iluka Coastal Life'. There was even a school! A school labelled 'Educational Facility for Children of Resort Staff'.

'What is this?' she gasped, and he beamed.

'The whole thing's the Iluka Health Resort,' he told her. 'What else?'

'I don't...'

'You don't understand?' He lifted the plans and folded them away, then took her firmly in his arms again. 'Amy, your stepfather put caveats on all this land—except the bluff. The caveat on the bluff simply says that it's to be used as a nursing home. But he specifically states that the nursing home is to be built as a resort. Now, my lawyer and I...'

'Your lawyer?'

'Henry,' he told him. 'Malcolm's father. We spent a bit of time looking at resorts on the internet, and nearly every resort we found had shops. And swimming pools. And lots of commercial extras. The big ones even had medical facilities. We looked a bit further and we found resorts like this one will be. A health resort with an acute-care hospital and all the ancillary things. Pharmacies, physiotherapists...you name it, we can have it here. Your stepfather left enough money to build the nursing home itself, but as it is it's not a real resort. So we approached the bank.'

'You approached the bank.' Amy was almost speechless.

Joss beamed. 'Yep. I even wore a tie, and Henry came, too. They were really nice to us. Especially when Henry outlined the financial foundations this place is built on. You have a mansion worth millions and a great nursing home and incredibly valuable land—and you own the lot.'

'But—'

He was brooking no interruptions. 'You know, in six years you stand to be an obscenely wealthy woman. This place is worth a fortune, and it'll be worth much, much more if you develop it. And with what's here already—the climate, the place—Iluka is the best place in the world to recuperate in. We'll attract clientele from around the globe.'

'But I can't afford—'

'Yes, you can,' he told her. He was holding her then, cradling her in his arms and enjoying her confusion. Or enjoying just holding her. Life had been cruel to this woman for far too long. This was his gift.

As Amy was his own sweet gift.

'We've done our homework and the bank sees this as a really viable investment,' he told her. 'It won't all be done at once, but as every stage works out we'll go on to the next. We have provision for a wonderful little town, whose main industry will be a state-of-the-art health resort. Its centre will be the hospital. This place is a gold mine, and the finance people agree. The bank will do very nicely out of it.'

'I don't understand.' She was so confused she was almost speechless, and his enjoyment grew. This felt...wonderful!

'We'll attract medical people from everywhere,' he told her. 'In fact, we already have. This district is screaming for decent medical facilities. When the council builds a new four-lane floodproof bridge and improves the road to match...'

'A bridge?'

'The council's agreed to build a bridge, and they've already negotiated government assistance. They see—like me—that this is a goer. And it is! Amy, I've already sounded out four doctors who have been aching to find somewhere like this to settle. So far there's two physicians, an anaesthetist, a gynaecologist—and me. We have everyone behind us. The government authorities are more than eager to have a major medical centre established in this area but until now they haven't had anywhere that would attract doctors. Doris in Bowra is so overworked she's near to collapse and she almost fell on my neck when I ran this plan past her. So...' He smiled and held her back at arm's length. 'How does that sound? For a beginning?'

'I...' She stopped, unable to go on. 'It sounds unbelievable.'

'It's not.' Joss's eyes were lit with excitement, aching to share his wonderful dreams with her. 'It's entirely believable. And workable. As part of the resort we'll build smaller cottages to house all the new workers, plus specialist houses for people like Marigold and Lionel who need help but want to stay in their own homes. We'll build a huge workshop for activities—we've even designed a shop-front for it so that Lionel can sell his kites and all those matinée jackets can find a home. Anything that's part of the resort can be as commercial as we like. By the way, the place will be big enough to need part-timers—volunteers—so people like Marie and Thelma will be able to do as much or as little as they like. Oh, and Malcolm...'

'Malcolm?' Amy was no longer breathing. She didn't need to. Who needed to breathe with this joy?

'I've spent some time with Malcolm in Sydney,' he told her. 'He's recovering but he's one very sorry boy.'

'As he should be.'

'Charlotte's been to see him, too, and laid his future on the line. If he wants to marry her then he comes to live here because Iluka's full of people who care. That's what she said. And he's desperately worried about how you'll take it, but...'

'But?'

'Well, the man is a decent accountant, even if he is a dope where relationships and boats are concerned. In fact,' Joss said grudgingly, 'despite his dopiness where boats are concerned, he's really quite clever. He worked out all the financial stuff. We do need a competent accountant, and he's incredibly excited about the project. So if you think you can bear seeing him again...'

'Why could I not bear to see him?' She was breathing again, but the joy within was threatening to overwhelm her. 'Why on earth not?'

'He betrayed you.'

'He betrayed Charlotte and she loves him. If she can forgive him, who am I to be judgemental?'

'You don't still love him—just a little bit?' He was looking anxious. That was crazy, Amy thought jubilantly. Crazy.

'How on earth can I love Malcolm—when I love you?'

'You love me?'

'I'd better,' she said. 'If you're going to be Medical Director and cut ribbons then I don't see that I've got a choice but to stick around.'

'You're going to be Director-In-Chief, and you can cut ribbons, too.'

'I thought I got to hold the handbags.'

'I'll leave my handbag at home,' he said magnanimously. 'If that's what it takes.'

'Gee, thanks.'

'But it could work.' He was still anxious, she thought. He was gazing at her with all the hope in the world. Like Bertram asking for someone to give him a ball.

No.

Not like Bertram.

Like Joss, asking her to give him a future.

She closed her eyes, and when she opened them he wa
still looking at her with hope.

'Amy?'

'Mmm?'

'Will you marry me?'

There was a long indrawn collection of breath and Amy
glanced toward the doorway. How many heads could fi
around one door?

'Can I have a puppy?' she asked.

'Ten.'

'Can I have a baby?'

'Ten.'

And she was laughing, joy and love and wonder all strug
gling for supremacy.

Love won. It always did.

'Of course I'll marry you,' she told him as he gathered he
into his arms and held her close. 'Of course I'll marry you
Oh, my love... Now and for ever.'

The entire population of the Iluka nursing home broke int
applause—and Amy and Joss didn't even notice.

Iluka was as it should be.

Almost as soon as the new bridge was built people started
drifting toward Iluka. There were things going on here. Jobs
were being advertised. Construction was starting on the new
hospital.

People came and saw and fell in love.

The day had been sun-soaked and beautiful. Families were
packing up on the beaches. The ice-cream van had closed for
the day. There were elderly couples walking on the beach,
catching the last of the sun's rays.

It was the end of another glorious day in paradise, as a
cluster of Iluka's long-term residents stood on the sand to
watch Joss Braden and Amy Freye exchange their vows.

'Come prepared for wet feet,' the wedding invitation had
stated, because Joss and Amy knew where they wanted to be

married. So this motley assortment of wedding guests hoisted their skirts and rolled up their trousers. Their bare toes were soaking in the shallows.

Amy and Joss stood on their rock above the waves, and the last of the sun fell on their faces as they faced each other with love. And certainty.

And joy.

'Do you take this woman…?'

'I do.'

'And you, Amy. Do you take this man…?'

'I do.'

There was such love here. Who could not wish this couple all the joy in the world?

In the last few months they'd transformed Iluka into the paradise it had always promised to be. There were a few disgruntled millionaires, but even they had been known to wander down when no one was watching and buy an ice cream from Mr Whippy. Their children played with Lionel's kites on the beach.

One of Lionel's kites was flying now.

No. Not one. Two of Lionel's kites. Huge box kites, being manoeuvred by children on the beach. They must have been primed by Lionel, because Lionel himself was knee deep in water, holding hands with Marigold, and beaming and beaming.

Everyone was there.

Daisy and David. Charlotte and Malcolm and tiny Ilona— Charlotte holding tight to Malcolm with a proprietorial air that said Malcolm had better not put another foot wrong if he knew what was good for him.

The look on his face said he knew very well what was good for him and he'd found it right here.

Bertram was here, though he wasn't venturing out into the water. He had enough to contend with—a brand-new springer spaniel puppy was trying to chase his tail and the dogs were spinning in circles of delight in the sand.

Who else? So many. Mary, Sue-Ellen, Marie, Thelma, old Robbie who'd been installed as head gardener—all the people they loved were here. It was just perfect.

The ceremony was over.

'I now pronounce you man and wife.' The celebrant beamed as Joss lifted Amy into his arms and kissed her.

'My wife,' he whispered. 'My love.' The whole world seemed to hold its breath as their kiss sealed their vows.

Above their heads the kites intertwined—only now there were three. Three box kites spun against the sunset, each painted crimson with huge white lettering. They'd been painted in an act of love from all the residents of Iluka Nursing Home.

One spelled Joss.

The second spelled AMY.

The final kite spelled FOR EVER.

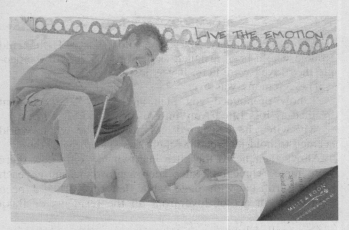

Modern Romance™
...seduction and
passion guaranteed

Tender Romance™
...love affairs that
last a lifetime

Medical Romance™
...medical drama
on the pulse

Historical Romance™
...rich, vivid and
passionate

Sensual Romance™
...sassy, sexy and
seductive

Blaze Romance™
...the temperature's
rising

27 new titles every month.

Live the emotion

MILLS & BOON®

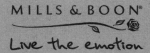

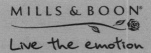

MILLS & BOON

STEPHANIE LAURENS

A Season for Marriage

Available from 18th July 2003

*Available at most branches of WH Smith,
Tesco, Martins, Borders, Eason, Sainsbury's
and all good paperback bookshops.*

0703/135/MB67

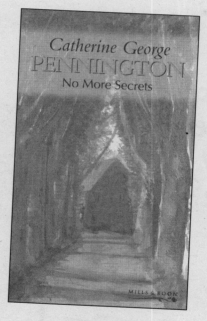

Don't miss *Book Twelve* of this BRAND-NEW 12 book collection 'Bachelor Auction'.

Who says money can't buy love?

On sale 1st August

Available at most branches of WH Smith, Tesco, Martins, Borders, Eason, Sainsbury's, and all good paperback bookshops.

BA/RTL/12

4 FREE
books and a surprise gift!

We would like to take this opportunity to thank you for reading this Mills & Boon® book by offering you the chance to take FOUR more specially selected titles from the Medical Romance™ series absolutely FREE! We're also making this offer to introduce you to the benefits of the Reader Service™—

- ★ FREE home delivery
- ★ FREE gifts and competitions
- ★ FREE monthly Newsletter
- ★ Exclusive Reader Service discount
- ★ Books available before they're in the shops

Accepting these FREE books and gift places you under no obligation to buy, you may cancel at any time, even after receiving your free shipment. Simply complete your details below and return the entire page to the address below. *You don't even need a stamp!*

YES! Please send me 4 free Medical Romance books and a surprise gift. I understand that unless you hear from me, I will receive 6 superb new titles every month for just £2.60 each, postage and packing free. I am under no obligation to purchase any books and may cancel my subscription at any time. The free books and gift will be mine to keep in any case.

M3ZEE

Ms/Mrs/Miss/Mr ....Initials.....................................
                                                                    BLOCK CAPITALS PLEASE
Surname ....
Address ....
....
....Postcode....................................

Send this whole page to:
UK: FREEPOST CN81, Croydon, CR9 3WZ
EIRE: PO Box 4546, Kilcock, County Kildare (stamp required)